ESCAPE TO EGYPT

BOOK TWO
OF THE

Lost Legend Trilogy

Written By

J.L. *Hardesty*

Illustrated By

Phyllis *Waltman*

PUBLISHED BY

J-FORCE
PUBLISHING COMPANY

Escape To Egypt

First Edition

ISBN 0-9701493-0-1
LCCN 00 091707

Cover Painting by Phyllis Waltman
Illustrations by Phyllis Waltman

Published by:
J-Force Publishing Company
Post Office Box 773632
Steamboat Springs
Colorado 80477

Editor
Marlene Bagnull

Technical Advisor
Joel Schulman

*The characters and settings in this story are creations
of the author's imagination and may not conform
exactly to accepted assumptions about
appearances and customs of the period.*

*THE LEGEND is another matter ~ its assumed
truth or fiction, the purview of the reader.*

Printed in Hong Kong
by Pacific Rim International Printing,
Los Angeles, California

To My Children's Children,
Cyndi, Kylie, Megan,
Zachary, Keith, Cole, & Michael

Heartfelt thanks to all the friends
& associates whose help & prayers
continue to be utterly invaluable assets ~
These friends include but are not limited to:
Marlene Bagnull, Kathy Goyak,
Christine Testolini, Joel Schulman,
Fr. George Schroeder, Sandy Emberland,
Tom & Kathy Conlon, & from Pacific Rim,
Lori Aliano, Cathy Davidson & Celine Chow.

Most of all, I thank my husband,
Jim Lauter, for his loving support,
his faith in God ~ & in me ~
& for his wonderful creativity.

Special Thanks
to
Michele Pfeifer
& Buddy Simmons
and to
Sr. Fernando de Santibanes
Dear & treasured
friends of the heart ~

PROLOGUE
Prologue

From the days of long ago, a story of immense consequence has been handed down, generation to generation. It is the account of a boy of great courage and two horses of great heart who, together, encountered the Christ Child and through Him, took part in the greatest story ever told . . . Thus began THE LOST LEGEND OF THE FIRST CHRISTMAS, BOOK ONE of THE LOST LEGEND TRILOGY.

In Book One, Michael, the young son of a Wise Man, was separated from his parents. The boy's mother, Junia, died in a plague and his father, Archanus, was forced to flee the Roman army that sought him for a crime he did not commit. For the boy's safety, his father placed him in the care of his mother's people, the finest horsemen of their time. Before the father and son parted company, Archanus shared with Michael the prophecy of a Savior who the Wise Men believed would soon be born . . . a birth that would be marked by the ascendance of an awesome Star.

"Look for me when you see the Star," were the Wise Man's last words to his son.

For many years thereafter, Michael lived with his mother's people, learning well the horsemen's ways in preparation for a great commission these good people understood would be his to undertake. Then one dark night, Michael was visited in a dream by an angel who told him that it was time for him to embark upon a most important pilgrimage.

PROLOGUE

Prologue

The next day Michael set off aboard the loyal mare, Lalaynia, with his supplies packed carefully on the back of the aged war-horse, Ghadar. When the wondrous Star appeared on the horizon, the expedition became, for Michael, a passionate quest for reunion.

Navigating by the light of the newly visible celestial guide, the boy and his horses continued the pilgrimage toward a destiny that would alter the history of the world, forever. In Bethlehem, the travelers arrived at that place beneath the tail of the Star where the prophesied Savior had been born. In the poignant, suspended moments following his arrival, though he did not meet his father as he had longed to do, Michael gained new peace and hope, and renewed faith to sustain him for whatever lay ahead.

Afterward, not comprehending fully the miracles he had just witnessed, Michael rode off in search of his father with the three Wise Men who had come to worship the newborn King. What the young horsemen did not realize was that his own purpose in God's grand scheme had not yet been fulfilled. In fact, his mission had just begun. Come along, won't you, as we ride with Michael on the continuation of his journey . . .

CHAPTER
One

CHAPTER One

The first light of dawn spread its glorious wings beyond the eastern horizon. Lalaynia and Ghadar snorted and stomped their feet, impatient to begin the day. Michael brushed their shining coats and sang a soft song to calm himself as much as to quiet his horses.

Reclining near the morning fire, Balthazar, Melchior and Gaspar, the three Wise Men who Michael had met beneath the Star, calmly discussed their plans.

"By nightfall tomorrow, we should reach the Great Sea," said Gaspar.

"Perhaps," commented Melchior, "but we still should not travel in haste. It is far more important that we avoid contact with other travelers."

"This is true," said Balthazar. "For more than a month we have varied our paths to avoid detection. We cannot suddenly tire of this scheme and thereby take a chance that someone will reveal our route of travel to Herod's henchmen."

From a few yards away, Michael could hear the conversation, and as he listened, his impatience increased. Leaning close to Lalaynia, he breathed in deeply, savoring the sweet musk of the mare's body, trying in vain to blot out the heavy stench of his companions' camels. The young horseman had no use for the plodding dromedaries. He understood that the Wise Men had chosen these creatures to bear them and their treasures across the arid Arabian Desert because the animals could travel for extended periods without water. But on this journey, there would be no shortage of water, so in the boy's eyes, the camels were an unnecessary burden. To him, they were lazy and stubborn, a source of incomprehensible annoyance.

Aching to find his father, from whom he had been separated for five painfully long years, seventeen-year-old Michael was too anxious about the potential reunion to travel patiently. The slow pace of the camels and the Wise Men's preoccupation with not being seen made the situation almost unbearable. Constantly, Michael had to hold the horses back . . . or repeatedly circle around in an exhausting effort to remain in close proximity to his fellow travelers. The strain of this tedious process kept the horses forever prancing and working themselves into a lather. Today, at the thought of the toll this exercise was taking on Ghadar and Lalaynia, Michael could hold his tongue no longer. Walking purposefully toward the morning fire, he rehearsed what he felt he must say.

"Michael, we have something to discuss." Balthazar's kind face creased in a smile as he welcomed the young man who now looked so much like his father, Balthazar's old friend and fellow Magi, Archanus.

"Good morning," the boy said politely, his brilliant blue eyes meeting the kind and intelligent eyes of the Wise Man.

"I too would like to talk with you . . . but please, you speak first."

The Wise Men nodded at one another, looking pleased and making Michael feel as though his attitude of respect had been recognized and appreciated.

"Last night," Balthazar began, "after you had fallen into a fitful sleep, we considered your plight. We know that you can scarcely abide the slowness of our camels. We understand how excited you are to proceed with all possible swiftness toward reunion with your father."

Running a hand self-consciously through his thick, dark hair, Michael allowed his gaze to stray for just a moment toward the inscrutable camels that stood chewing their morning meal.

"We cannot modify the speed with which we travel," Balthazar continued, "until such time as we exchange these persevering beasts for the horses that will be both more eager and more fleet of foot."

"Please forgive me," Michael interrupted, feeling as though these perceptive men had read his thoughts. "I have meant no disrespect."

"There is no need for apology," the slender and dusky Melchior chimed in. "You have done nothing wrong. You have been most patient in an impossible situation."

"We will all be well served if we separate for a short time," Balthazar added.

"We know that you can avoid contact traveling alone even more easily than you would if you remained with us." Gaspar, the youngest and most stoutly built of the three Magi joined the conversation.

"But where will we meet again?" asked Michael, suddenly regretting his impatience.

"We can rejoin one another in Joppa," said Balthazar.

"Perhaps you will meet your mother's people along the way," Melchior said in a hopeful tone.

"That would be a good thing." Michael brightened. "I can obtain fine horses for you if I find my uncle."

"That may not happen since the horsemen so rarely winter in Egypt," said Balthazar cautiously.

"There are horse traders in Joppa," Melchior interjected. "And one way or the other we can procure new mounts for us all. Then we can continue together on our crusade to locate your father."

"Thank you," Michael responded, confused by his feelings, and yet determined to move on. "I will not disappoint you again."

"At no time have you disappointed us," said Gaspar. "We understand that each man must do what he must to satisfy the call of the One God."

"Do not be too surprised or unhappy if things don't work out exactly as you expect them to," added Balthazar, echoing the admonition he had made before the travelers departed from Bethlehem.

Vaguely recalling those earlier words, Michael brushed aside the memory and prepared for his departure. On Ghadar's back, he carefully packed the supplies his friends insisted he take. Surprised by the sadness he felt at this parting, Michael kept his face turned toward the horse, surreptitiously brushing away his tears. Then, rushing lest they detect his emotion, he bid the Magi a hasty farewell and turned to ride away.

"Keep your hope strong in the One God," Balthazar called after the departing figure. "He will not forsake you."

"We need to find water soon," Michael said, patting Lalaynia's neck. It was the end of a long day in which Michael and the horses had covered much ground. For several hours they had been following the dry and narrow path of a ravine that cut between the mountains. No sooner had he uttered his concern than an inviting oasis appeared before him. "I don't know why I ever worry when you're in charge," he laughed, stroking Lalaynia's neck again and shaking his head in wonder.

As though pushed back by an unseen hand, the mountains separated and made way for a broad clearing. Sweet clover and grass shared the meadow with spreading sycamores and willows that grew up around a bubbling spring. The song of the waters and the breeze in the trees welcomed the exhausted travelers. When he finished caring for the horses, Michael ate a sparse meal, then spread his blankets beside the spring and lay down for the night.

The sliver of sky above the canyon was dense with stars, but no moon relieved the darkness. A peaceful stillness enveloped the clearing, wrapping its arms around the companions who enjoyed its refuge. Soon, in the pleasant darkness, Michael fell into a deep and healing sleep.

Far into the night, the atmosphere began to change. Though no sun or moon breached the blue-black sky, a mysterious light warmed the chilly air and Michael began to stir. There was no breeze, no movement of night creatures, still, some secret sound broke the silence. Beneath the trees, Ghadar and Lalaynia stood calmly alert. In spite of the fact that it was not yet morning, Michael tossed restlessly as if being awakened by the dawn.

After a while, unable to descend back into the comfort of deep sleep, he sat up and looked around, anxiously seeking the source of the light and the music that sang to his spirit though it remained somewhere beyond his hearing. Yearning to heed the mystic call, the young horsemen started to rise from his resting place. But an ethereal hand held him still.

"Have no fear. I will not harm you," a resonant voice commanded. "I bring a message from the One God."

Recognizing the presence, though he had no clear recall of any previous meeting, Michael shook off the last vestiges of sleep. "Who are you?" he asked, looking into the mysterious brilliance beyond which he could not see.

"It was I who spoke to your father when you traveled with him long ago. And I am the one who warned the Wise Men to depart from Bethlehem by another route following their adoration of the Christ Child. I have traveled with you many miles, guided and protected you often."

"Why have you never revealed yourself to me before?" Michael asked. "And why do you hide from me now?"

Out of the circle of light, a huge being appeared. Hair the color of wheat crowned a wide forehead. Amber eyes were set deep above high and angular cheekbones. The nose was smooth, aristocratic. A benevolent expression softened the face above a strong chin and jaw line. Wings were folded behind immense shoulders. Muscular legs supported the powerful body, and mighty arms relaxed at the sides of this being Michael now recognized as an angel.

The young man could only stare in wonder. In spite of the angel's extraordinary size, nothing about him was fearsome. Dazzled and bewildered, Michael was surprised to find his own voice.

"Why have you come to me? Always before you have whispered to me . . . and to the others I know . . . in dreams. Why have you honored me this time with your presence?"

"Your mission is not finished," replied the angel, "and

the One God felt that you would better understand its importance if I spoke to you directly this time."

"I don't understand." Michael shook his head in confusion. "I have never understood . . . even that night in Bethlehem when all of time seemed to stop. Nothing about my mission has ever been clear."

"We are not always given to know the plans of God." The angel's voice was firm, but gentle. "I can only tell you what He would have you do now."

"What am I to do?" Michael asked uneasily.

"You must go to Jerusalem as quickly as you can. The wicked King Herod has learned of the Magi's duplicity. In his anger, he has ordered all of the boy children under the age of two years to be put to death."

"But why?" Michael gasped in horror. All he could think of was the Child in the manger beneath the Star. For long moments he could not speak. His heart pounded as if to leap out of his chest. Sweat beaded on his previously cool forehead.

"The Child, Jesus, whose birth you attended, is the Son of God, sent to bless all of His earthly children," the angel said. "Herod fears the loss of his own power because he has heard that the Boy born beneath the Star is the prophesied Savior who will one day be called the King of the Jews."

This confirmation of the Child's divinity served only to frighten Michael further. "But what of the Magi?" he asked, fearing also for his friends and chastising himself again for having left them. "What have these good men done to anger Herod?"

"In their innocence," the angel began, "the Magi went to Herod's palace to inquire about the birthplace of the King, whose Star they had been following. Of course Herod knew of the Prophecy and seized on this chance to find the One he feared. He bade the Wise Men to continue their journey and to return to him when they found the Child, pretending he too wished to worship the Babe."

"But you warned them to depart by a different route, and they have gone into hiding," Michael said.

"Yes," replied the angel.

"I still don't understand what I can do to help," Michael heard himself saying. "There is awful danger . . . I do not fear for myself, but for the Child and His family. They deserve a powerful army to protect them. I am only one horseman. I have neither the skill nor the strength to fight Herod or his soldiers."

"Nevertheless," the angel said, "you have been chosen to provide safe passage for Mary and Joseph and the Child. If you heed the call, you will take this Holy Family into Egypt where you will remain as their protector until it is safe for them to return to their homeland."

"How will Balthazar and the others continue their journey without the fresh horses I am to provide?"

"Do not fear for your friends. They will find their way to the horse traders and beyond. After all, have they not traveled a lifetime without you?"

"How arrogant of me to think otherwise." Looking embarrassed and still apprehensive, Michael paused. "Please forgive me," he continued at last. "I don't mean to be selfish when I have been called to such noble purpose. But I must ask . . . what of my father? Will I ever see him again, or am I destined to travel without him forever?"

"One day you will be reunited. For now, you have been called to carry out the most important mission of all time. Will you obey?"

"Yes, of course," Michael whispered, his young mind overwhelmed with fear that he might fail at this auspicious task as his heart reached out for the faith and obedience that had been his father's greatest bequests.

"This is as the One God hoped it would be," said the angel, turning as if to depart.

"But wait," Michael's voice was filled with alarm. "Please don't go without telling me how I will find the family. We left them in Bethlehem. How will I know where to look in this other town of Jerusalem?"

"You will find them at an inn near the temple," the angel said, and then he was gone.

The next morning, for the first time since they departed from Bethlehem with the Magi, Lalaynia and Ghadar were cooperative and enthusiastic about the direction of their travels. They no longer stomped or pranced in discontent. Instead they lowered their graceful necks and moved forward with determination, covering twice the ground in one day that they had traveled, even without the camels, the day before.

As the shades of night began to descend, Michael thought he should look for a place to camp, but Lalaynia moved on. Insisting they stop at a water crossing, Michael got off of Lalaynia and bent to refresh himself before checking both of the horses for signs of fatigue. Torn by the urgency of his mission and concern for the health of his horses, he hesitated, looking up hopefully, as if the encroaching darkness might hold for him some answer.

Not long past twilight, the glowing, cerulean sky still hid the stars, and a cool breeze drifted across the land. Somewhere in the distance a night bird called to its mate. Lalaynia and Ghadar tossed their heads and snorted impatiently. Understanding that the animals had answered his question, Michael swung back up onto the mare and allowed her once more to set the pace.

On a hillside at the southern edge of the valley, a Roman cavalry unit was making camp for the night. Only one of the soldiers saw the boy and the horses gliding silently through the evening . . . and that man, Octavian, chose to keep what he had seen to himself.

⨳   MEANWHILE . . .   ⨲

Near the city of Antioch, in a land far to the north, a man lay struggling in that dark place between life and death. . . .

"He was so much better, and now . . ." Pain and confusion filled the eyes of the handsome boy who sat applying cool compresses to the man's fevered brow. "I do not understand what has happened."

Long shadows fell across the room. A slender man paced back and forth, shaking his head, seemingly lost in thought. In the doorway stood a young girl looking on, her eyes bright with tears. Two slaves waved giant fans to keep the air in the sick room from becoming stagnant.

"Are his wounds not healing?" asked the boy, impatient for an answer. "Is there something inside that we cannot see?"

"Mi . . Mic . . . Michael . . ." The voice of the man on the cot was ragged and reedy.

"He has been calling for his son," said Luke sadly. "If only Michael were here, perhaps his father would again find the will to live."

"Archanus is a man of great strength and hope," said Keptah. "He could not have survived the robbers' attack had it been otherwise. He has not given up, nor will he. You too must have hope. Nothing is impossible with the One God."

"I will share your hope," said Luke, firmly. "I will not leave his side until he is well."

CHAPTER
Two

CHAPTER *Two*

Meanwhile, in the land of Judah, Mary and Joseph, the earthly parents of the Child born beneath the Star, prepared for His dedication to God. On the eighth day after His birth, the Baby was circumcised and given the name of Jesus. Just over one month later, when the time of Mary's purification was completed in keeping with the Law of Moses, Joseph set off with his family on a journey to the temple in Jerusalem where the dedication would take place.

As Joseph led the little donkey that carried Mary and Jesus through the dusty streets of Jerusalem, heads turned to watch their progress. Shopkeepers and Roman soldiers, women and children, workmen, pious Pharisees and Saducees~all were drawn to the travelers, though none could say why. Unfashionably clothed and obviously poor, these pilgrims presented no grand spectacle, and yet, about them there was a mystical air of grandeur and nobility. The fine particles of dirt that rose up in their wake shimmered like gold in the sun, and the subtle illusion further mesmerized the onlookers.

Joseph was a tall man whose broad shoulders could support much. His hazel eyes mirrored the goodness of his spirit and the kindness of his heart, while his unique size and the determination of his gait gave him an imposing presence and disguised his gentle soul.

His weathered hands and suntanned face showed that he was a workman who preferred the out-of-doors to any form of confinement. But his appearance did not speak of his exceptional intelligence, nor did it tell of his devotion to the God of his fathers, known to those outside the Jewish faith as the One God.

"We're almost there." Reverence filled Joseph's voice as they neared the temple.

"Yes," Mary whispered.

At the sound of her voice, the big man turned to drink in the wonder of his young wife and the Baby she had miraculously conceived.

Mary cradled the Child gently in her arms. Riding sideways on the donkey, she looked up from the face of Jesus into the eyes of her husband. Silken tendrils of golden-brown hair escaped the blue cloth that covered her head. Her huge, doe-like eyes, fringed with the thickest of dark lashes, nearly matched the color of her hair. Her nose was small and delicate, her generous lips almost always parted in a sweet smile.

A slender woman, Mary was so physically lovely that from earliest childhood, she had been the target of much jealousy and contempt. Before her betrothal to the much sought after bachelor, Joseph, Mary was often scorned for her studious nature and deep religious devotion. Of the women who knew her, only Mary's mother and her much older relative, Elizabeth, forgave her for her rare beauty and unwomanly intellect.

Now, as Mary and Joseph made their way toward the temple, only Joseph's great stature and obvious power protected his comely wife against the lustful advances of the city's rougher male element. Ignoring the open stares of all those by whom they passed, the man headed purposefully toward the temple.

⁘

Inside the temple, on the terrace between the Court of the Gentiles and the Court of the Women, an ancient man known as Simeon sat, still and quiet. The long shadows of afternoon crossed the man's brow and softened the creases of his aged skin. His once blue eyes were rheumy now, almost transparent. The hair of his head, as white as the marble of the temple, mingled with his beard and lay in weary profusion on his chest. Though he had spent much of his life in the temple's inner courts, Simeon chose now to sit near the women and the Gentiles, who he believed were often more faithful to God than were those allowed beyond the Wall of Separation.

In the gathering dusk, Simeon sat peacefully, his mind lingering on the special promise he had received several days earlier as he lay on what he believed to be his death bed. A man of less faith might have dismissed the mysterious visitation as a hallucination born of his dying. But Simeon had spent his long life studying the teachings of his religion and communing with his God. So, when the Holy Spirit of that God came to him, he listened, and he believed.

That afternoon, like this one, was warm and soft. The sense of renewal that lives in the very air of early spring enveloped Simeon in its gentle hope. His east-facing bedchamber had surrendered to the approaching dusk until all at once a light so glorious and brilliant that it defied description took possession of the small space and its inhabitant.

"For all the days of your life you have been God's righteous and faithful servant," said a voice from within the light. "Now, as the time of your passing draws near, He wishes to reward you."

"But I seek no reward," Simeon protested. "I have lived as He has led me to live, and I have been richly blessed."

"And you will be further blessed." The radiance pulsed with life as the words entered Simeon's heart. "I am the Holy Spirit of God. I have come to tell you that you will not die before you have seen the Lord's Christ . . . the Son of God."

"I have prayed my whole life for this moment," the old man whispered in a ragged voice. "But for many weeks I have not been able to leave this bed for my legs can no longer carry me. How will I, then, witness this miracle?"

"You will be given the strength you need to go to God's temple. There you will await the presentation of His Son."

"Am I called to some service?" the old man asked hopefully.

"You will speak to all those present who respect you and understand the depth of your knowledge." Joy over Simeon's willingness to serve emanated from the Spirit. "You will tell them that this Child is the Messiah of whom their prophet, Isaiah, spoke."

"But how will I . . ."

"You will know Him." Then, before Simeon could speak again, the Spirit was gone.

With incredible renewed vigor, Simeon rose from his bed, left his comfortable home and the care of his family, and took himself into the temple courts.

❦

In the temple, not far from Simeon, a woman of his age knelt in prayer. A warm ray of saffron sunlight peeked over the temple wall, parting the shadows and creating a pool of light that surrounded her.

"Dear, dear Anna, sweet daughter of Phanuel," Simeon whispered. "You, more than I, deserve to see the glory of this Lord who has come to save our people."

The aged prophetess did not glance in Simeon's direction but raised her eyes to the light. For just a moment Simeon could see, beneath the weariness, the face of the lovely young girl Anna had been when she married one of his kinsmen so long ago.

"Only seven years as a wife," he thought, "then never another husband and no children to brighten your days. How you must have suffered . . ."

Then, as if she had heard his thoughts and responded, Simeon was filled with a strange peace. All at once, he knew eighty-four-year-old Anna, who had spent most of her days and nights in this very temple worshipping God and sharing His truths with others, was among the most blessed of all.

Like a mountain of marble and stone, Herod's temple rose majestically above Jerusalem. Five hundred cubits square, the noble edifice reigned supreme over all Judea, its aspect mysterious, resplendent and powerful. The lowering sun rested on the cedar roof of the colonnades that surrounded the temple. The amber light of eventide gave life and form to the stark white of the Corinthian marble columns that supported the roof. Within the temple, shadows chased the sunbeams of day's end from the lower level courts toward the pinnacles above.

As the splendid monument at last came into their view, Mary and Joseph were overwhelmed with awe. "I rejoiced when they said to me, 'Let us go to the house of the Lord,'" said Joseph, pausing to savor the grandeur before him.

Not far from the temple gates, Joseph found a small tree beneath which he could tether the donkey. He helped Mary down from the little animal's back and placed his arm around her as they moved toward the entrance to the temple. Into the cool portico the husband and wife walked, hand in hand, then moved on to the Court of the Gentiles where querulous merchants bartered and hawked their wares. Casting her eyes downward and pulling her Child closer, Mary looked away from the sellers of turtle doves and pigeons who shouted above one another, cajoling the faithful to obtain their sacrificial birds, each promising the greater purity of his own wares.

As he approached the merchants, Joseph thought of the weeks he had spent in Bethlehem, working to earn the money needed for the customary sacrifice. Now, with the meager coins that filled his pouch, the loving husband purchased a pair of doves.

Relieved to escape the hubbub, Joseph led Mary past the pillars where signs in Greek, Latin and Hebrew warned the Gentiles to come no farther under penalty of death. When they had climbed the stairs and reached the Gate called Beautiful at the next level of the temple, Joseph stopped for a long moment. Overcome once again by the awesome power of the place, he recited from memory the words of King David, "Our feet are standing in your gates, O Jerusalem."

Then together they spoke the words that are the heart-cry of all who know and worship the One God. "Pray for the peace of Jerusalem. May those who love you be secure. May there be peace within your walls and security within your citadels." They stood for a few quiet moments, their heads bowed in prayer, before proceeding across the Women's Court toward the Court of the Israelites that Mary could not enter.

Climbing the semi-circular steps that led from the Women's Court to the Gate of Nicanor, Joseph felt suddenly alone and frightened. His joy at the prospect of dedicating the Child to the Lord was overshadowed by his feelings of personal unworthiness. "How can I be all this little One needs me to be?" he asked the sky that was open above him. "O God . . ." Joseph's distress was released on a breath heavy with emotion, "I am not a man great enough for the responsibility You have given me."

Though the sun was low, the motionless air within the temple remained hot. From just inside the Court of the Israelites, Joseph, carrying Jesus, looked back at Mary who watched from her place on the stairway at the west side of the Women's Court. He paused, confused by obedience to his religion and his desire to share this occasion with his wife, before turning to approach the priest.

Cradling Jesus in one strong arm, Joseph looked up hopefully at the man who would bless this precious Child. Without so much as a glance at the believer who now knelt before him, the priest began to intone the standard blessing. In the droning voice of one who knows the words, though he has lost the essence of their meaning, the priest muttered the dedication of the Child, then indifferently dismissed the tall peasant as was his way with people he considered to be of lowly status.

Joseph barely heard the words and had no sense of the priest's misplaced disrespect. For as the man spoke, the Spirit of God whispered to Joseph's great heart, "Peace,

Joseph. My peace I give to you . . . a gift that comes with everything else you will need to be My Son's earthly father. Do not fear, but rejoice that you have been chosen. You will be well equipped for all that lies ahead."

Strengthened by new hope, Joseph walked with his head held high toward the place where Mary waited. At the entrance to the Women's Court, he placed Jesus gently in His mother's arms. With their eyes on the Child, the couple turned to leave the temple. But just before they reached the Court of the Gentiles, they were stopped by a man whose upright bearing denied the age that was evident in his eyes.

"Please," said Simeon, "do not go until I have looked upon this precious One."

Joseph glanced around in wonder as, from all over the courtyard, people began to move toward them. Some came because the respected elder who had sat so long in the shadows was now standing. Some were inexplicably drawn toward the scene, while others merely followed their neighbors to see what was causing all the commotion.

As the crowd gathered, Simeon gazed with reverence upon the Child still held tenderly in His mother's arms.

"May I?" he asked Joseph, nodding toward Jesus.

Not answering, Joseph looked to Mary who nodded and placed her Son in the outstretched hands of the old man.

Stepping into the broadened circle of light wherein the prophetess Anna still knelt, Simeon raised the Child high above his head and spoke in the deep and sonorous tones of a man much younger. At the sound of his voice, a hush fell over the crowd. Even the spiritless priest in the inner chamber ceased his droning liturgy.

"Sovereign Lord," Simeon thundered into the surrounding silence, "as You have promised, You now dismiss Your servant in peace. For my eyes have seen Your

Salvation, which You have prepared in the sight of all people, a Light for revelation to the Gentiles and for glory to Your people Israel."

The spectators began to murmur among themselves.

"How can this be?" asked one.

"These people are nothing but rough peasants," another said disdainfully.

"Hush!" a powerful voice ordered. "This is Simeon . . . one of our most honored elders. How dare you question his wisdom and his veracity."

"Please bless these parents and give them strength for that to which You have called them," Simeon continued, ignoring the crowd.

"This Child is destined to cause the falling and rising of many in Israel, and to be a sign that will be spoken against, so that the thoughts of many hearts will be revealed." As he spoke, Simeon's eyes flashed as blue and ardent as they had been in his youth. Then he turned to gaze with tender mercy upon the young mother. "And a sword, dear Mary, will pierce your own soul."

At those words, as if to protect his wife from their portent, Joseph moved closer, supporting Mary with his own strength, then looking courteously toward Simeon. But the old man had finished and was handing the Child to the prophetess, Anna, who had come to stand beside him when he first began to speak.

Giving thanks and praise to God, Anna spoke of Jesus at length to all that looked forward to the promised redemption. "This," she said in a clear, strong voice, "is the Savior for whom our people have waited since first His coming was predicted by the prophet Isaiah."

Again, members of the assembly began to talk, some questioning, some assured.

"Where is the thunder and lightning?" one asked.

"This can't be the One for whom we wait," scoffed another. "There would be much pomp and circumstance at His coming."

"Anna and Simeon are too old," a mean-eyed woman added. "They know not what they say."

A stoutly built young man who had studied for many years with Simeon parted the crowd and took his place beside his old teacher. "You will all be still or be forever accursed," said the man. "Simeon and Anna are the best among us and they have been given to know the Truth of God."

"Some will believe," Anna said calmly. "Others will be lost." Then, for some time, the old woman continued to testify to the divinity of Jesus.

At last, Anna placed the Babe in His mother's arms. No words passed between the two women, yet Joseph had the feeling that a deep understanding had been exchanged. The crowd did not follow when Joseph led Mary to the donkey that stood waiting beneath the tree. All at once exhausted by the events of the day, the husband was grateful to be left alone to search for a place where he and his family could rest that night and he could ponder all that he had heard.

❦

Mary and Joseph took into their hearts all that was said about Jesus in this holy place. In the years ahead, they would often recall the words of Simeon and Anna. And, watching Jesus grow to manhood, they would be comforted by this memory and reminded of the Child's singular origin. Always, they would accept the mystery that was Jesus, understanding that He must fully experience life as a human being in order to fulfill His destiny.

In fevered delirium, Archanus tossed and moaned. Now and again he would utter some unintelligible word or phrase. But for the most part, there were only the sounds of his anguish.

Luke remained at the sickbed, keeping up a silent vigil. When Keptah entered, Luke could find no words and only looked up with imploring eyes at his teacher.

"His injuries are improving, but now the lung sickness threatens him," Keptah said, bending low to place his hand on the sick man's forehead.

"How could this have happened when we worked so hard to make him well?"

"This is not your fault, Luke. You could have done nothing more. His body is so depleted by the battle to overcome his wounds that he has no strength to fight off this illness."

CHAPTER
Three

CHAPTER
Three

That night, Mary and Joseph found shelter at a nearby inn. Though Mary slept lightly, alert to her Child, Joseph fell into a deep, exhausted sleep.

No dreams came to Joseph during the first watch of the night. Then, all at once, he became restless, tossing and turning on his mat, muttering unintelligibly. Sitting nearby with her Son in her arms, Mary watched with concern as her husband struggled to awaken. Finally, he sat up, his face a mirror of apprehension.

"I have been visited by an angel," he said. "The same one, I think, who has come to us before."

"What has he told you?"

"He said I must get up and take you and Jesus away from here. We must leave, at once, for Egypt . . ."

"But why?" Mary asked. "What has happened?"

"The evil King Herod fears that Jesus will one day take over his kingdom. Even now, soldiers are searching Bethlehem, bent on murdering the Child."

"How will we escape?" Mary gasped.

No sooner had she spoken than they heard a knocking on the door. Mary fell to her knees in prayer, fearing that the soldiers had already found them and praying for God's protection.

"It cannot be the soldiers," Joseph said, more hopeful than assured. "There is not enough noise, and they would not be so polite."

"Joseph," a young man's voice whispered through the wide crack between the door and the wall. "I have been sent to help you."

Crossing the room and peeking out through a knothole in the door, Joseph recognized the horseman who had come to them with the shepherds and the Magi just after Jesus was born. Unlatching the door, he bade Michael enter.

"How did you find us?" Joseph asked.

"I cannot explain this any more than I can say why I have been chosen. I only know that this is the place to which the mare, Lalaynia, has brought me. Once here, I was drawn to this door."

"I believe that you have been sent by God," Joseph said. "There is no need for further explanation."

"Come," Michael said, his tone gentle. "The horses will take us to safety."

"Our God is good." Joseph said. "On the heels of the angel who came to warn us, He has sent the vehicle of our deliverance."

"We must hurry," cautioned Michael. "Herod's soldiers are a murderous lot. I have had occasion to flee from them before."

Mary looked deeply into the blue eyes of the young man who stood before her and saw into his heart. "We are grateful," she said simply.

"There is a cart filled with supplies behind this inn," Michael said. "Somehow I know it was left there for our use."

While Michael and Joseph hitched Ghadar to the cart, Mary knelt beside her Child and said a fervent prayer, giving thanks and asking for protection. Jesus lay on his back, arms outstretched as if in benediction. A lock of Mary's lustrous hair brushed across her Son's face as she looked beyond Him toward the mare. "Again, He reaches out to you," Mary whispered. "How good it is of God to send such a wondrous creature for our deliverance."

Carefully, Michael and Joseph helped Mary into the cart, placing Jesus in His mother's arms. Once Joseph had climbed in beside his wife, Michael covered the precious cargo with rugs given him by the Magi, swung onto Lalaynia, and signaled for Ghadar to follow.

As they made their stealthy way through the streets of Jerusalem, Michael was alert and vigilant. Startled by every movement, every sound, he felt the same awful fear that had gripped him when he and his father escaped the Roman soldiers so many years earlier. But this time, the responsibility was his. His father was not there to make decisions, to tell wise stories, or to console.

This was also different from his journey beneath the Star, when there was no one to worry about except himself. On this dark night, there was no Star to light the way. On this fearful expedition, he anticipated no reunion. This night, he was responsible for the safety of a man, his wife, and the most important Child the world had ever known. The knowledge of this responsibility was almost more than Michael thought he could handle.

Shortly after they left the inn, they were accosted.

"Halt!" The sharp command shattered the predawn stillness. Michael signaled his horses to stop.

Three soldiers stepped out of the shadows. One roughly grabbed Ghadar's bridle, another Lalaynia's, while the third took Michael's arm and jerked him down off the mare's back.

"What are you doing sneaking through these streets at night?" growled the soldier still holding Michael's arm.

"I am just a poor trader," said Michael respectfully. "I am on my way to sell my rugs to the merchants of this town."

"Answer, now! Why do you travel these streets at night?"

"I lost my way and was late arriving . . ."

"What are your goods?" asked the soldier holding Ghadar's bridle.

"Rugs, sire . . . they are rugs from the east."

"Let us see if there is something here that would please our captain," said the one who had pulled Michael from Lalaynia's back.

"Wait . . ." Michael was verging on panic. "Let me choose the richest of my wares and present them to you . . ."

Shoving Michael aside, the soldier nearest him moved toward the cart.

Suddenly a great wind rose up from the dusty street. Almost in unison Ghadar and Lalaynia reared and pawed at the air. Two soldiers fell beneath the animals' striking hooves. The third raised his arms as if to protect himself from blows that Michael could not see. Lalaynia nudged Michael and he swung onto her back. Without waiting for encouragement, the two horses leapt into a gallop. Tails flying, nostrils flared, they dashed through the streets with the cart barely touching the ground behind them.

Michael did not look back. His heart pounding and his hands shaking, he leaned forward as though he could help Lalaynia to move faster. Behind and all around them the wind roared, but they cut through the night unscathed. In the cart beneath the rugs Mary and Joseph clung to one another and the Child and prayed unceasingly to the God of their fathers for deliverance.

In the wake of that near disaster, Michael realized that he was once again being guided and protected by the same angelic army that had accompanied him ever since he left the horsemen. Fairly flying toward the edge of town, Michael whispered a prayer of thanks to the One God for the angels He had sent to fly on the night wind beside him.

Once Jerusalem was well behind him, Michael began to feel a veil of serenity descend upon the land. As the moon and stars disappeared into the encroaching morning, Lalaynia settled into a long, easy trot, once again seeming to know where she was going and confidently leading the way back into the hills west of Jerusalem. Each evening, Lalaynia chose a place to rest and eat.

Three days later, at the Wadi El Arish, where that river emptied into the Great Sea to the south and west of Gaza, the travelers met the horsemen, who welcomed Michael and his companions with much rejoicing . . . and none of the questions that might have been asked. That evening, Joseph sat near the night fire with Michael and his mother's brother, John, the leader of the horsemen.

John's wife, Sarah, visited with Mary, while Joseph, Michael and John shared stories of their recent travels. Michael told his uncle all about his journey following the Star, about the angels who had traveled with him, and the grave responsibility he had for the well being of Joseph and his family.

"I am sorry that we cannot remain with you," Michael said to John late that night, as the men prepared to retire.

"We understand," John replied. "You have been called to a great purpose and we will help you any way that we can."

"Thank you," Michael and Joseph said at once.

"One thing we can do," said John, "is to keep old Ghadar and Lalaynia with us and send you off with two fine young geldings~one for you and one that Joseph can drive to pull the new, larger wagon we will provide,

"I am grateful," Michael said, "but I cannot let go of Lalaynia. Though I will miss him, I know that Ghadar will be happy with the herd, and I will be glad to have one of the young geldings you offer. Only Lalaynia must stay with me. When we have settled in our new home, Lalaynia will become a companion to Mary, and the gelding will become my mount."

"As you wish," John said smiling. "I had chosen two geldings and I will present you with the best of these. His name is Esdraelon. He will serve you long and well."

"I would ask you another favor," Michael added.

"Anything."

"Balthazar and the other two Magi who attended the birth of this Child are preparing for their trek to the land north of the Great Sea where they think they shall find my father. I was to meet them in Joppa and provide them with horses for the journey. Can one of the horsemen make this meeting in my place and present the Wise Men with some of our finest mounts?"

"Of course," said John generously. "Tomorrow you and I will select the horses and your cousin, Matthew, will depart for Joppa without delay."

❦

Only two days after they had joined the horsemen, Michael and the Family resumed their journey.

The handsome young Esdraelon stood between the traces of Mary's cart, pawing at the ground. Joseph sat on the driver's bench holding the reins to keep the big bay from walking off. Lalaynia stood with her muzzle resting in Mary's outstretched palm. A veritable sea of horses spread out across the plain and in its midst stood a young man, his arms around the neck of an old, black gelding, silent tears coursing down his sunburned cheeks. As if to comfort him, Ghadar reached around and nuzzled Michael.

Standing alongside the cart, John and his wife, Sarah, looked into the herd and saw their nephew. "Another goodbye," Sarah said softly. "He is so young to have known so many partings." No one spoke again until Michael returned. His expression was somber, but he was composed as he swung up onto Lalaynia.

"I wish that I could tell you where we're going," Michael said to his aunt and uncle, "but only the angels, and this sweet mare, know our destination."

"It would not do well for us to have that information, even if you knew," John answered, looking up at Michael with eyes that mirrored his own anguish. "We will meet again, of that I am certain," the older man said, clearing his throat in a weak effort to disguise his emotion.

Sarah reached up and took Michael's hand in hers. Then, finishing her husband's thought, she said, "When it is safe, we will find our way to you."

Lalaynia moved away, then, leading the way toward a future none could yet imagine. John and Sarah stood hand in hand watching until the travelers were little more than tiny specs on the horizon. Then they turned and walked toward the herd and their own tomorrows.

Under the watchful eyes of those who cared for him, Archanus stirred on his cot. In dreams he rode beside his son, their thoughts linked, their horses keeping step with one another.

"He is improving," said Keptah. "His lungs no longer rattle with the sounds of death and his fever has begun to recede."

"But he is still so weak," said Luke. "And it has been so long since you found him near death. Will he ever be the strong man he once was?"

"We can only hope that he will recover fully," answered Keptah, thinking back to the fateful day when this dear friend departed to follow the Star. He had argued with Archanus that morning, advising the Wise Man not to make the journey alone. But Archanus insisted that he must go in search of his son . . . and the Savior.

"I promised Michael that we would meet again at the coming of the Star," Archanus told Keptah that day. "Never have I broken a promise to him."

"Why did I let him leave alone?" Keptah asked.

"Because he would have it no other way," said Luke. "You have counseled me not to feel guilt. Now I say the same to you. Don't forget, had you not decided to follow Archanus, he would have died on the road that very night."

"I wish I could take credit for that decision." Keptah shook his head. "But you must recall it was the angel who sent me . . ."

"And you must recall what you have taught me well . . . that we can always choose to ignore our angels, but your choice was to obey."

"You are an apt student," said Keptah, a smile lighting his eyes. "Now you must continue using the healing skills that you have learned to help the One God bring Archanus back to us."

CHAPTER
Four

CHAPTER *Four*

O n the twentieth day of their journey, the little company crossed the Nile into the Land of Goshen that would be their home for a time. The travelers had been outside Herod's dominion for several days and could have settled in a place closer to home. But, as though Lalaynia knew that Joseph and Mary would languish in a dry and barren land unlike that from which they hailed, she brought them to a lush and verdant plain where the waters were plentiful and the climate as gentle as their own.

For his family, Joseph set up a tent beside a running stream, then began the task of making mud bricks and building a small dwelling. Michael pitched his tent on a mesa overlooking the home of his friends, setting himself up as their sentinel.

Though it was customary for families to settle in small towns for safety and convenience, Joseph chose to establish a home place for his family a slight distance away from the nearest community.

"We'll be safe and comfortable here," he said to Mary and Michael. "In the towns, people are too curious and there is not enough privacy. We have plenty of water and space to grow our own food. We can be happy here." No one argued.

The horses wandered at will between the two homes and the days passed gently. As they settled in, Mary and Joseph did not ask if Michael would remain with them. They merely treated him like a member of their family, letting him know in word and action that he was loved and appreciated.

"Lalaynia is with child," Mary said one day as she served Michael and Joseph their noon meal.

"I wish that were true," Michael said, "but she has been barren for three seasons. She was the best producer in the herd . . . then the foals stopped coming. That was one of the reasons she was sent with me on my earlier journey."

Mary smiled and said only, "Surely she was with a stallion before you departed, and the result will soon present itself."

"The time is right," Michael said, looking with love at Lalaynia. "She could have been with Zadir, the herd sire, shortly before we left the horsemen for the first time. But how dangerous these expeditions were for an older mare that was carrying a baby. What if I had robbed her of the chance to bear another foal?"

"As it happens, you robbed her of nothing," said Mary, glancing down at the Child in her arms, then turning her gentle gaze back on Michael. "You and Lalaynia and the other horses have done God's will. He has protected all of you from the start and He will continue to do so. Have faith. You are among His chosen."

As he often did in the presence of this mother and her Child, Michael felt set apart from the earth, in a dream, with every sense heightened and the air alive with mystery.

During the ordinary course of his days, Michael thought rarely of this Child's divinity. It was only at moments such as this that he brought to mind what his father and the angel had told him about the Savior whose birthplace would be marked by a miraculous Star. And then, with logic creating a barrier between his heart and his head, it was difficult for Michael to see this seemingly helpless Babe as the Prince of Peace his father had so long awaited.

"I must go and tend to the other animals," Michael said finally, turning away. As he walked toward the stream, the battle within him raged on and the faith that lived in his heart could not overpower the rationalization that governed his mind.

"May You bless all his days," Mary looked to the heavens and prayed, "for he was the willing instrument You used to deliver Your Son from the hands of the enemy. Please fill him with wisdom and teach him that truth and logic *can* live together. Open his heart to Your Son and bless that heart with Your peace that surpasses all understanding."

Michael stopped near the horses. And all at once, in answer to Mary's prayer, God moved. Michael's resistance was torn away. His own will set aside, he was overcome by a force so powerful that it rendered him helpless. His strength drained, he staggered, then fell to his knees, his head in his hands, unable to speak.

A wave of darkness washed over him, captured his mind, tumbled it through the relentless undertoe of forgetfulness and remembrance. When he emerged, his whole body tingled, like the aftermath of a sharp blow to the knee or the elbow. But with this sensation, there was no pain, only heightened awareness of the life force vibrating within him. Again, black velvet obscurity swallowed him and he nestled deep in the cool blindness of its embrace.

After a while the light began to dawn, silent as a stealthy cat, patient as the opening of a bud, the warmth of clarity approached and enfolded him. Like a blurred kaleidoscope, colors blended and separated and united to form new shapes, soft edges fading toward unclouded messages.

He did not so much awaken as he came forth, rose up from a deep and secret place where hearts are met by knowing and sentience imbues the soul.

Gently, peace took possession of him, and he began to pray. "Thank You, thank You," he breathed, his tone soft, passionate.

He knelt for a time in silent communion with the One God, and the world waited, utterly still. The horses did not stir. The breeze paused from its lithe dance through the grass. The steady rolling stream hesitated, and the clouds suspended their journey across the sky. In the trees, the birds were hushed, while the creatures of the meadow remained motionless, at calm attention.

Then exultant words of thanks and praise began to escape Michael's lips while tears of joy coursed down his suntanned cheeks. While he was praying, a vision of Jesus as an Infant, then a Boy, and finally a Man, appeared before him. In Jesus' unwavering gaze, pure love, without condition, revealed itself, then reached out to envelop Michael in its ultimate power. In that moment, he understood that Jesus would be the heart of all his tomorrows . . . that the peace of God had found its way into the deep recesses of his heart . . . and that never again would he ever be alone.

Brilliance manifested itself, surrounding the brothers, suffusing the air with benevolence and comprehension. From this day forward, though he would remember sorrow, Michael would no longer feel its crippling pain. Forever after, he would call to mind the face of Jesus, and the memory of this epiphany would come to life, offering strength and courage . . . and always the purest, truest love.

For all the days of his life, the horseman would carry with him a sense of resurrection, of having been born anew, of oneness with Jesus in a brotherhood that would never end.

❧

Three months later, an anxious Esdraelon, stomping and snorting beside him, awakened Michael. "What is it, my friend?" Michael said to the tall bay, getting up to follow the animal even as he spoke. Esdraelon jogged down off the mesa, leading Michael to the grassy clearing beside Mary and Joseph's house. There in the moonlight stood Lalaynia, her soft muzzle exploring the neck and the withers, the back and the loins of the most magnificent black colt Michael had ever laid eyes on. So new to the world that his shining body was still wet, the foal was already on his feet, challenging the night into which he had so recently emerged. Beside Lalaynia stood Mary, her face alight with a mother's serenity.

"It's a miracle." Michael grinned. "How did you know?"

"Sometimes God tells me when miracles are coming," Mary said softly.

Plopping down in the grass near the mare and her foal, Michael shook his head and laughed aloud.

It was many days later before the horseman finally allowed himself a full night's sleep. He feared predators, sickness, any number of catastrophes that could rob the world of this precious colt. In the excitement that followed the marvelous birth, he forgot about the angels who had protected him and his companions for so long, mistakenly thinking that he, a mere mortal, had to be in charge and to somehow keep things under control.

During that night when he finally rested, the now familiar angel came back to him with a promise. "Because of your obedience," the angel said, "you will be rewarded . . . and all those who love horses after you will share in your prize.

"This colt, who you will name Zabbai because he is a gift from God, will be the founder of a dynasty. His sons will be kings of the wind, running faster than any other horses in the wide world. His daughters will have such rare beauty that kings and queens and other royalty through all of the ages ahead will covet them. Three strains of great-hearted horses will be the fruit of Zabbai's loins . . . and from your place in heaven, you will see and be proud."

"But what am I to do?" Michael asked. "How do I care for him? Where do we go from here? Do I return him to the horseman? He is theirs, after all."

"This colt belongs to no man," the angel said patiently. "He will stay with the Son of God for now. They will grow together, and no creature on the earth will ever be as richly blessed as is this horse. One day the horsemen of your mother's family will bring their mares to him and his dynasty will begin. You must simply be at peace, knowing that the Father of the Child, Jesus, who slumbers in His mother's arms, will care for both of these youngsters, preparing them for their missions even as He prepared you for yours."

"So am I to leave now? Is my assignment completed?" Michael asked, hurt plain in his voice.

"Have you forgotten?" asked the angel. "You are to stay with the Family until it is safe for them to return to their homeland. In the meantime, you will continue to be their protector."

"But what of my father?" Michael asked. "When will I be able to go in search of him?"

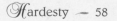

"I do not know," replied the angel. "I have only been told of this mission. Beyond this, we must await further enlightenment."

☞ MEANWHILE NEAR ANTIOCH ☜

"I am sorry to have awakened you," said Luke, removing the compress from Archanus' forehead to dip it into the cool basin of water and herbs. "You were calling for Michael again and I did not wish to disturb your dreams."

"I will not soon see my son," Archanus whispered, his voice still weak, though his heart had begun to beat with renewed strength.

"How can you be sure?" Luke asked.

"An angel . . ." Archanus began before drifting once more into fitful sleep.

CHAPTER
Five

CHAPTER
Five

he days and years passed gently on the Nile Delta to which Lalaynia had brought Michael and his adopted family. The Child, Jesus, grew and became strong; He was filled with wisdom, and the grace of God was upon Him.

From the time of Zabbai's birth, when Jesus was still a Babe in arms, the colt took to Him like no other. Poor Lalaynia, the sweetest and most solicitous of mothers, seemed constantly aggravated by her willful son. While she grazed, Zabbai would wander to the cottage to be near Jesus and Mary. If they were inside, the colt would wait near the door until Mary brought Jesus outdoors to be near him. When they were together, Zabbai would frequently nuzzle the Child's soft hair and His belly, as if checking to be sure that his Boy was all right. Often, Mary, carrying Jesus, would go with Lalaynia to the field when the little mare seemed too distressed that Zabbai wouldn't leave Jesus behind to follow her.

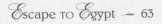

Before Jesus could walk, Michael began putting Him on Lalaynia's back and teaching Him to ride. Zabbai stayed always right beside his mother and her passenger, acting as if the honor of carrying this Child should belong only to him.

※

"Zabbai wants to carry Jesus," Mary said one day shortly before the colt's third birthday, when Michael was getting ready to take Jesus along with him on Esdraelon for a ride down to the river.

"Zabbai isn't old enough to carry anyone." Michael's tone was amiable. "I need to ride him first, to make him gentle enough for Jesus. What kind of a horseman would I be, what kind of a protector, if I endangered the Boy's life and Zabbai's limbs by trying too soon to satisfy the silly colt?"

"I don't think he's silly." Mary laughed. "I think he knows his job and is anxious to do it."

"Perhaps . . . It's hard not to ride him; he's so big and so pushy. But my mother's people would never forgive me if I damaged his young legs or his back by riding him too soon. We must all be patient."

"Why not just let Jesus sit on him?" Mary asked.

"What if the colt spooked?" Michael worried.

"You don't really think he would do that with Jesus on his back," Mary chided.

"Well . . . maybe not. Another day, though, not now . . ."

Finally, one afternoon not long after that conversation, Michael gave in.

※

In the carpenter's shop he had built behind their house, Joseph worked patiently, first cutting and shaping the pieces of a chair, then fitting them together and securing them. When that job was finished, he would spend hours sanding the chair, then rubbing it with the oils that would preserve it and give it a rich luster. Wanting to help, though he was unskilled at Joseph's craft, Michael had assumed the responsibility of obtaining the raw wood from which Joseph made his furniture and of delivering the finished products. Just back from one such errand, Michael watched with admiration as Joseph plied his trade.

"How rewarding it must be to have such skill," Michael said.

"Your ability with the horses is no less than mine with wood." Joseph looked up from his labors and smiled at the young man who had become to him like the best of friends and the dearest of brothers.

Just then, a happy Jesus came bouncing through the door. Joseph caught the Boy up in his arms and tossed Him high above his head, setting aside his work to join in the Child's merriment. Right behind Jesus, Mary hurried in, breathless from the game of hide-and-seek she had been playing with her Son. She did not apologize for the intrusion but merely added her own sweet laughter to the music of the moment.

From his place beside Joseph's workbench, Michael watched, the smile on his face hiding the ache in his heart. Once, his father and mother had shared this same sort of joy and playfulness with him. Perhaps, if his mother, the beautiful horsewoman, Junia, had not passed away when he was just twelve years old, he would not have had such a painfully empty place within his heart. But as it was, no day went by that Michael did not think of his mother with lonely regret. So, while the beauty of the relationship between Mary and Joseph and Jesus reminded Michael of the best times of his life, this loving bond also touched that sorrow which now, for the most part, lay buried deep within him.

Wriggling in His father's arms, Jesus reached for Michael. Joseph set the Boy down and put his arm around Mary. Leaping into Michael's arms with the trust known only to little children, Jesus laughed with glee and asked, "Can we ride today?"

Trying to discard his sad thoughts, Michael hugged the Child. Jesus leaned back in Michael's arms and placed His two small hands on either side of the young man's face. Blue eyes met and the love of the Boy embraced the heart of the man.

"How does He touch my spirit with just a look?" Michael wondered, relaxing into the sense of well-being that washed away his momentary sadness. Gratefully, he gave Jesus another hug, then set Him on His feet and said. "Today you will ride Zabbai."

"Zabbai?" Jesus' eyes lit up. "Really?"

"Yes, really." Smiling, Michael reached out to tousle the Boy's hair, but Jesus was too quick and He had already taken off in a happy dash toward the horses.

"How blessed we are to see Him grow and to love Him," Joseph said to Mary as they stood together watching Jesus dance off toward Zabbai.

"I'll be careful with Him," Michael called back over his shoulder.

"We're not worried about that," Joseph and Mary said in unison.

By the time Michael caught up with Jesus, the Child was already trying to climb up Zabbai's front leg and onto his back. For his part, the big colt stood still as stone. His only motion was to stretch his long neck around and place his muzzle against the Boy's back to keep Him from falling.

"Wait for me!" Michael called. Even though he understood the amazing bond that existed between horses and young children, he couldn't help but worry. As he picked Jesus up and placed Him tenderly on Zabbai's back, Michael's thoughts traveled back to the days when he was a little boy, no older than Jesus, sitting at the feet of his mother's geldings while they grazed. He recalled how the big horses had moved carefully around him, never placing him in any danger. He remembered when his mother had first allowed him to ride alone, instead of in front of her on her horse.

"Can we go now?" Jesus asked, breaking into Michael's reminiscence.

"Not yet," Michael said patiently. "I want to put a halter on Zabbai with some reins for you to hold onto."

"We don't need those," Jesus said, His little Boy's voice sweet, but sure.

"Dear God . . ." Michael said, letting out a great breath and looking skyward. "Somehow I know You'll protect this Son of Yours . . . and this horse. But please, can You help me keep breathing when I forget You're on the job?" Michael smiled as he spoke, pleasantly surprised by the ease with which he had just addressed the One God and the peace this spontaneous prayer had given him.

"Wait for me, all right?" he said to Jesus. "I'll get Esdraelon and we'll ride together."

That was the beginning. From that day on, Jesus rode Zabbai for hours every day. The Boy's balance and His timing were perfect. When He sat on Zabbai, it was as though they were one. No matter the gait, the action, or the speed, the little body of the Boy melded with the great back of the horse. And Jesus was right, He needed no bridle to guide the big colt. With a thought, a subtle shift of balance, a small pressure from His short legs, Jesus told Zabbai where He wanted to go. They made the most beautiful picture Michael had ever seen . . . of freedom, made sweeter by love and absolute devotion.

✣

It became customary for Jesus and Zabbai to accompany Michael when he went out to obtain wood or make deliveries. Sometimes, Mary even rode along on Lalaynia, or drove the cart filled with goods so that she could visit with the woman of the house while Jesus played with the children. Occasionally, Michael conversed with the men while Mary and Jesus socialized. But more often he stayed near the horses, keeping a protective eye on the Boy and His mother.

Mary especially liked to go along when they made deliveries to the home of Nathan, a merchant who lived nearby. Michael regularly delivered furniture to Nathan's house rather than traveling the greater distance to his store in town. Mary and Nathan's wife, Lidah, had liked each other at once and become fast friends in no time. Jesus, on the other hand, wasn't so quick to become comfortable with Nathan and Lidah's sons.

"Come," Mary beckoned her Son on their first visit. "Let Michael take Zabbai with the other horses for a drink while you meet Lidah's boys."

Reluctantly, Jesus slipped down from the safety of Zabbai's back and pressed Himself closely up against His mother. At four years old, He hadn't spent a great deal of time with other children, and when He met someone new, it always took Him a while to warm up. Lidah's boys, on the other hand, knew no shyness. At the arrival of these visitors, they came running, giggling and shouting playfully, until a look and a shake of the head from their mother told them to calm down.

"Thomas, Nathaniel and Marcus, this is Jesus," Lidah said, when she finally corralled the three rowdy boys. "He is our neighbor. Make Him feel welcome."

The ten-year-old, Thomas, was the oldest and the quietest of the three. Walking toward Jesus, he said, "Come on out to the river and play with us."

But Jesus' attention had been captured by something less threatening than a bunch of noisy boys. In the shade beside the house, a mother dog lay nursing and cleaning a litter of furry pups.

"Would you like to hold one?" asked Lidah.

"No thank you," Jesus answered. "I'll just watch them for a while."

"He'll come in a few minutes," Lidah told her boys. "Let Him visit with the pups here in the quiet, before He has to get used to your noise."

The brothers busied themselves then, playing tag and showing off, trying to entice their shy guest to join them. Michael watched from a short distance away. Having felt similar discomfort as a child, the horseman thought of a way to help Jesus relax and to encourage Him to play. They had a favorite game, a kind of peek-a-boo, hide-and-seek where Michael would pretend to sneak up on Jesus. Then, meeting Michael's challenging smile, the gleeful Child would dash away merrily.

As Michael advanced, Jesus responded in the usual way. Turning reluctantly from the pups and forgetting to be frightened of the other children, Jesus tucked His head behind Mary, then peeked out and laughed loudly before darting away toward the meadow. The chase was on and before they knew it, Lidah's sons had joined in. It wasn't long before all the children were romping and tumbling in the grass together, while Michael stood back watching the frisky game.

"Wanna come to the river now?" asked Thomas. "There are some frogs and ducks down there. And sometimes we catch some fish for lunch."

"Sure," Jesus said, taking the hand that Thomas offered. "I like to talk to the frogs and the ducks."

By the time the boys returned to join their mothers and Michael for the afternoon meal, they too had become fast friends. Standing back in his own quiet way, Michael wondered at the ease with which Jesus made friends after He got over His initial shyness. For Michael, there had been no childhood companions except his mother and the horses. He had always been the loner who stood back and watched the other children at play, never joining in. He was glad that Jesus didn't share his reticence, that He could be a regular boy . . . in spite of His difference.

That night, Thomas sat with his mother as he sometimes did after the other boys had fallen asleep. "I think that Jesus is . . ." he started hesitantly, "well, different than us." Thomas paused again, scratching his face and looking to his mother for an answer to his unasked question. When she didn't say anything, he went on, "I think He is special. . . . you know? He can talk to the animals! I know we all do that sometimes, but when He says something, they seem to listen. . . . and they come right up to him. . . . the frogs and the ducks. . . . even the birds. They all just gather around Him like they're waiting for Him to tell them something." Thomas paused again and smiled at his mother. "And did you see how the puppies took to Him? Especially the littlest one."

Lidah sat quietly, looking up at the night sky, letting Thomas ramble on. She allowed her sons time to think things through before she offered her ideas or opinions. But this time, there was more to her silence. This time, she too had perceived something beyond the normal in all three of the people who visited her home that day. Finally, she said, "I think we shouldn't look too hard for differences. Let's just try our best to be their friends."

"Okay," Thomas said with some reluctance. "But Mother, when the puppies are old enough, can we give the little one to Jesus?"

"Of course," Lidah said, putting her arm around Thomas and pulling him to her. "As long as it's all right with Mary."

When she finally went to bed, Lidah thought back to part of the conversation she had with Mary while the boys played and the handsome Michael looked on. "The horseman is very cautious," Lidah had remarked. "He says little, but seems to see all. If his eyes weren't so gentle, he would look very fierce in the way he protects you and your Son."

"He is our protector," Mary had answered simply.

"I wonder what they fear," Lidah thought as she prepared herself to retire after saying good night to her oldest and best loved son. "I could see that Mary wanted to share more with me, but she was too cautious." Sighing, Lidah blew out the last candle and went to bed. "Maybe someday she'll tell me about her mystery," was Lidah's last thought as she drifted off to sleep.

⤢ MEANWHILE NEAR ANTIOCH ⤢

"Archanus is much better these days." Rubria's tone was more hopeful than certain.

"Yes," Luke smiled at his friend. *"And he loves to have you visit. You make him laugh when no one else can."*

"It is you he loves," Rubria touched Luke's cheek. *"You remind him of his son."*

CHAPTER
Six

CHAPTER *Six*

I n Egypt, life was good. Joseph established an excellent business. Mary and Lidah were the closest of friends, as were Jesus and Lidah's sons. The puppy, dubbed Shadow because he was as inextricably hooked to Jesus as was the Boy's own shadow, had become a new member of the Family and a beloved companion to Jesus. Michael enjoyed the work he did for Joseph and was even learning some of his friend's craft.

One late afternoon, two years after Jesus and Mary's first meeting with Nathan's family, Michael sat on his hillside thinking about the simple joys of his existence. Sometimes he missed the herd, and often he thought that Zabbai should be with the mares, siring fine foals, improving even the very best. Whenever such a thought crossed his mind, as it did at that moment, he marveled at the extraordinary beauty of the young stallion.

In the way of the horses that carried the world's rarest and most sought after blood, Zabbai, born black as night, would gradually lose that color, turning gray by degree, and eventually a pure, lustrous white. At the age of six years, the young stallion was the most perfect specimen of fine horseflesh that Michael had ever seen.

Zabbai's sleek coat was beautifully dappled, a rich multi-hued blue gray. His mane and tail were still jet-black. His head was exquisitely chiseled, his eyes huge and dark and wide set, the frame of bone around those eyes perfectly shaped and dry. His nostrils were so large as to appear perennially flared.

To accommodate the great amounts of air that he could drink in, his immense lungs and capacious heart were housed beneath a tremendous heart girth. Zabbai's neck was so long and flexible that had it not been set so high on his shoulder, he might have looked out of balance. The line from his ears to his arched tail was a perfection of smoothness and angle. His legs were longer and more elegant than the others of his line. The stallion was, Michael thought, power and glory personified.

For some reason, this train of thought led him to his sense of Jesus and the mild confusion that gently cluttered his mind, even when his heart remained clear. Though Michael fully understood his assignment to be that of an earthly guardian, he sensed a certain futility in these efforts as they related to Jesus. For, in spite of the fact that this Child behaved much as other children His age, Michael could not entirely separate Him from the glory of His birth and the ever present memory of that blessed event.

Since the loss of his mother and then his father, Michael had carefully distanced himself from other humans, believing that he could not bear to be abandoned~in any way~by anyone he allowed himself to love too much. He could not, however, maintain such a posture with any member of this Family. The love he felt for Jesus and Mary and Joseph was unlike anything he had known before. It was an infinite emotion, all-powerful and pervasive, that became his very impetus for existence. He felt at once like a protective father and a dependent child. Michael's world consisted quite simply of this Family and the horses. Beyond this realm of his mind, his heart and his spirit, he never ventured. Only that deep and ceaseless yearning for his father marred the landscape of Michael's mind.

"Have we lost you to your dreaming?" Joseph's friendly voice interrupted Michael's thoughts.

Looking off toward the east where the horses grazed, Michael had not noticed his friend walking up the western slope of the hill. "Welcome to my lookout." Michael smiled and stood to greet his friend.

"I don't come up here often enough," Joseph said. "I forget how much of the delta you can see from this hilltop."

In Joseph, Michael saw the same kind of strength he recalled in his father. Though at twenty-eight Joseph was only five years older than Michael, the younger man could not help making the comparison. It wasn't that their features were so similar; it was more their carriage, their demeanor. These unbidden thoughts crossed Michael's mind now as Joseph stood before him, the late afternoon sun warming his sun-darkened face.

"What is it?" Joseph asked.

Michael paused, embarrassed. "I was thinking of my father."

"And comparing me to him?"

"How did you know?"

"Mary . . ."

"She reads my mind sometimes," Michael said, his face relaxing. "She saw me watching you at work one day and asked me if you reminded me of my father."

"This is an honor for me . . ."

"But I am nearly as old as you are. Does this not insult you?"

Joseph laughed, then answered with a question. "When you last saw your father, how old was he?"

Michael thought for a moment. "I don't know, really . . . perhaps thirty."

"In your mind, he has grown no older. And in your heart you are still the boy riding out in search of the man you hold most dear. To be compared to one you love so deeply is a great honor."

"Thank you," Michael said, looking away to conceal the tears that had filled his eyes. "I too am honored by our friendship, though sometimes I am frightened by the weight of my responsibility."

The two men stood side by side, silent for a time. The sun had fallen beneath the western horizon, but its golden rays lit the evening, weaving themselves between the clouds, turning their downy underbellies voluptuous shades of pink and yellow, orange and amber.

Moved by the beauty before him, Michael asked, "When the One God has given us so much, how do we repay Him?" The question overflowed from Michael's heart and filled his eyes again with unbidden emotion.

"He does not require repayment," Joseph answered, understanding the origin of Michael's question, much as Archanus had once done, without requiring explanation. "He only commands us to love one another and to be as obedient to His will as it is possible for us to be."

"How do we know His will?"

"Simply ask that He reveal it. It is written that God gives us the desires of our hearts. I believe this has a double meaning. It is HE who places the truest and purest of our desires within us. And it is HE who fulfills those desires."

"God has given me the desire to protect and serve you and your Family," Michael said. "But, what if I fail Him?"

"Remember, if He gives you the desire, He will see that it is fulfilled. You will not fail. You have chosen to obey this great trust He has placed on you. He will guide you and sustain you and cause you to succeed."

"Joseph, Michael," Mary called from the foot of the hill. "Come and eat . . ."

Outside the house a table was set with lovely plates and water goblets that Nathan had traded to Joseph for some of the carpenter's handcrafted goods. Steam rose from a covered pot in the center of the table. A bluebird sat on the nearby window sill cocking his head curiously, chirping a message that only Jesus might have understood.

"Where is Jesus?" Michael asked, a note of alarm in his tone.

"He was with the horses the last time I saw Him," Mary said, smiling. "You don't always have to fear for His safety."

"I know." Michael looked embarrassed. "Maybe it's just that I've never entirely gotten over that feeling of being hunted that I first knew when my father and I escaped the Romans."

"There is no shame in your caution," said Joseph. "We must never forget that we are in exile because some of those same Romans may still be seeking to murder Jesus."

"I'm going to look for Him," Michael said, grateful for Joseph's understanding. "He should eat with us, and I won't be able to enjoy Mary's fine cooking if I don't know where He is."

Lalaynia stood grazing alone not far from the house. Michael patted her lovely neck then swung easily onto her back. "I need you to find the other horses, sweet girl," he said softly, urging her forward with a squeeze of his legs. As they loped toward the river, Michael was reminded of his early days with the horsemen when he spent hours alone exploring the countryside, traveling ahead of the herd or just getting to know a young horse that he was training.

Wondering why it was so difficult for him to give Jesus the same liberty and latitude that had been his own, he thought of the Boy's age. At six years old, Jesus was an enigma. On the one hand, He was wise far beyond His years, exhibiting an intelligence and knowledge that were all but incomprehensible. On the other hand, He giggled and played and frolicked like any child His age. He talked to the birds and the butterflies, holding them ever so gently in the palm of His hand or carrying them around on His head or His shoulder. Often, Jesus would sit beside the river and the frogs would gather round Him as if He were telling them fascinating tales. The goats that Mary kept for milking did His bidding without question and preferred His company to that of their own kind. Even the wild Ibis could not resist Him. His dog, Shadow, had become His constant companion and confidant. But it was with Zabbai that Jesus had the most miraculous bond.

As he rode out in search of Jesus, Michael pondered all of these things in his heart, admitting to himself that now and again he was struck by a pang of something like jealousy. His own greatest gift had always been his way with the horses, but in the presence of Jesus and Zabbai, he felt like little more than a rank novice. Zabbai loved and catered to Jesus in a manner that Michael had never before seen any horse behave. Up until this time, he had always prided himself on his ability to communicate with all horses and to elicit a rare and wonderfully loving response. But the greatest of his achievements paled in comparison to the relationship shared by Jesus and Zabbai.

All these thoughts drifted across Michael's mind as Lalaynia carried him toward her son, Zabbai, and his charge. Just as the horseman was beginning to think that this time his mare would not be able to locate the wanderers, the glorious gray stallion, his head high like a mighty sentinel, came into view. But where was Jesus? Michael wondered, and his alarm increased. Only when they drew nearer did Michael see Esdraelon standing behind Zabbai, and at the horse's feet, Jesus. Shadow lay nearby, his belly exposed to the cool sand, his head on his paws, his eyes following every move that Jesus made

The Boy's tunic was soaking wet and covered with mud. Streaks of reddish brown dirt decorated His cheeks.

"Is something wrong?" Michael asked, his relief vying for position with his concern.

"Hello." Jesus smiled up from His position on the ground beside Esdraelon. "The gelding's feet are very hot and sore. I am helping him to feel better."

"He's always been a glutton." Michael shook his head and knelt down beside Jesus. "I wish the horses didn't have to suffer so much more than we do when they overeat."

"Don't worry, the waters of the Nile and its cool mud will heal Esdraelon."

"How do You know this?" Michael asked.

"You have told me of your people's remedies."

"Yes, I suppose so," Michael said, unconvinced.

Continuing with His ministrations, Jesus packed mud all around Esdraelon's hooves, then sat cross-legged beneath the horse with His two hands wrapped gently, for long moments, around one hoof and then another. The slightest hint of steam rose from beneath the Boy's hands . . . and the bay rested peacefully, offering no resistance, his head low, his eyes half closed.

When He had completed this task, Jesus led Esdraelon into the river until the animal was knee deep. Then He stood stroking the shining coat while the water swirled around the gelding's legs.

"This will aid the healing," Jesus said to Michael.

"Yes . . ." Michael barely whispered, overcome by the sense of some miracle beyond the familiar treatment.

"You're a mess." Michael chided, shaking off the confusing sensation and addressing something simpler. "You need to clean Yourself up before we go back to enjoy Your mother's fine meal."

Jesus ducked His head shyly, then looked up at Michael, a sheepish little grin on His lips and in His eyes. "That's what rivers are for," He said, chuckling and diving into the deeper water, then popping up 20 feet beyond Esdraelon. "Come on in," He called. "The water is cooler out here . . . feels good! Come on . . . we'll dry on the way home."

Michael couldn't resist. He waded out past Esdraelon, dove in, then came up beside Jesus and directed a great splash of water at the Boy's happy face. They played water tag, swimming and diving and rolling around like a pair of otters, until all at once Michael realized how late it had gotten. On the bank, Shadow bounced up and down and barked. Then, just as the game was ending, he appeared to gain enough courage to dive into the deeper water and swim toward Jesus.

"We need to get back," Michael said, grinning at the dog swimming clumsily toward them.

"I'm sorry," Jesus said, hugging Shadow and burying His face in the dog's soft, wet fur. "I shouldn't have worried you and My mother. And now we're very late for the meal."

"She knows You're fine," Michael said, realizing the truth of his statement. "I'm the fool who always worries."

"You're no fool," Jesus said sternly. "You are a beloved child of My Father . . . and He doesn't take kindly to people saying bad things about His children."

"I stand corrected." Michael said affectionately. "I only meant that I should know You and Zabbai are capable of taking care of yourselves."

"Yes . . . but you never forget your mission."

"Thank You for knowing this."

As they waded toward the riverbank, Michael rested his left hand on the Boy's shoulder. In his right hand, the horseman held a long strand of Esdraelon's mane with which he led the animal.

While the gelding's back feet were still in the water and his front feet on the shore, Jesus knelt down and felt for heat in the hooves and the band of flesh just above them. "They're much cooler," He said, looking proudly up at Michael. "I think he'll be all right."

"I know he will," Michael said, recalling his earlier feeling. "But I think I'll still ride Lalaynia home and let Esdraelon follow."

Michael looked up, then, and saw a line of riders on a bluff beyond the river's western banks. Sunlight glanced off pieces of armor, and above the soft sounds of moving water, the sharp clanking of metal could be heard.

"Romans," Michael said, apprehension plain in his tone. "I wonder if they've seen us?"

"I don't think so," Jesus said calmly.

"Even so, I think we'll travel a little more quickly than we'd planned," Michael said, wondering how much Jesus knew, beyond what they both could see.

They moved into an easy lope and didn't slow down until they could no longer see the soldiers behind them. All the while, Michael kept a close watch on Esdraelon, studying

the way he moved to be certain he was in no pain. The horseman was grateful for the spongy delta soil and for the healing. Still, he worried for the safety of this good horse.

When they reached the house, Michael jumped down from Lalaynia's back and hurried toward Joseph.

"We saw a large cadre of Roman soldiers west of the river," he said anxiously. "Do you think they know of our whereabouts?"

"It's not likely," answered Joseph. "They're probably on some other errand."

"But what if they have come for us?" Mary asked, her voice and her eyes exposing her fear. "Remember what Herod did to the children in Bethlehem when he was trying to find Jesus?"

"Yes . . . of course," Joseph said, placing a strong arm around his wife. "We have tried not to live in fear, but perhaps it is time to be more vigilant."

"If the soldiers come this way," Michael offered, "we'll be able to see them from some distance . . ."

"Yes," Joseph agreed. "Then we can take steps to hide both Jesus and Zabbai."

"I don't know," Mary whispered. "I am afraid . . ."

"My Father is with us," Jesus said, taking Mary's hand and looking up at her. "He will not let us come to harm."

Michael turned at Jesus' words and was captured by the look of love and tenderness in the Boy's ancient eyes. The sense of peace that came to him whenever Jesus spoke with this strange sort of authority battled in Michael's mind with the more logical sense of fear that had tugged at him all evening. Finally, he said, "We should rest. We do not know what awaits us tomorrow."

Soft sunlight filtered through the leaves. A fountain sent its glistening waters skyward. Birds chirped noisily, and a breeze danced across the courtyard. A frail man rested in the shade of an olive tree. A lovely young girl sat nearby, playing with a puppy that bounced and frolicked in the unblemished joy of the innocent.

"My wife always wanted to give my son a puppy," the man said, his voice sad.

"Then why didn't she?" asked the girl.

"Our lives were not so simple as yours, sweet Rubria." The man smiled indulgently. "We moved often and lived too much in the confinement of the city where it is difficult for children, and dogs, to grow as they should."

"Sometimes I speak without thinking first." said the girl. "I know that you miss him terribly."

"Yes, I do." Archanus reached down and touched Rubria's cheek. "But you and Luke bring me great joy in Michael's absence . . ." His voice trailed off.

"What are you thinking?" asked Rubria.

"My son is a man, now," Archanus said sadly. "His boyhood is long passed. We missed so much . . ."

CHAPTER *Seven*

CHAPTER *Seven*

That night, neither Michael nor the horses could relax. Zabbai stomped and snorted restlessly. Esdraelon walked around and around, circling Michael's tent like a watchman on guard duty. Lalaynia stood with her head high, her ears forward, gazing across the delta, her full attention captured by something beyond the far horizon.

Finally, in the middle of the night, Michael arose. The stallion and the gelding came to him at once. But Lalaynia remained at her post, unwavering. "What is it, old girl?" Michael asked as he walked toward her. Stroking her neck, the horseman looked in the direction of the mare's gaze but could see nothing at all. Lalaynia pawed at the ground, then reached around and gave her man a nudge. "What do want?" Michael asked. "Is there something out there?" Again, Lalaynia reached for him, this time grabbing his tunic in her teeth and pulling gently. She continued to nudge him and paw restively until he gave in.

"All right," he said a last, unable to keep from smiling. "Let's go." Lalaynia shook her head and nickered toward the house where Jesus and Mary and Joseph slept. The tall young man swung up onto the back of the anxious mare. Once Esdraelon and Zabbai had jogged down the hill and reached the house, Lalaynia took off at a long lope.

With the wind in his face and sweet freedom in the air, Michael's mind wandered back to those lonely days when he only desired the companionship of the horses, when all that gave him surcease from his broken heart was the liberty he felt galloping into forever aboard a horse. He worried, now, that his heart had overpowered his mind, making him vulnerable because of his deep and abiding love for this Family that had become his own. When Lalaynia stopped abruptly beside the river and shook herself to gain his attention, Michael had lost track of time.

The night was still and dark. Only the sound of the Nile flowing toward the Great Sea, and an occasional movement or call from the creatures that lived beside the river, broke the silence. Lalaynia turned to the south, her head low, her feet barely touching the ground, and began a catlike advance through the rushes. Then, all at once, she stopped again, her ears tight forward, her nostrils flared, beckoning Michael to cautious attention.

A ribbon of smoke wafted up from behind the willows. Michael could hear deep voices murmuring between the intermittent sounds of horses on a picket line bumping against one another in the listless movements of their sleep. With barely a sound, he slipped down off of Lalaynia's back and began to crawl toward the smoke and the sound. Before he knew it, he was only a short distance from a Roman encampment. Gripped by fear, he caught his breath lest any sound could escape his lips and willed his heart to be quiet. Then, he settled into his hiding place and prayed for the soldiers to give away the reason for their mission.

His wait, though unbearably tense, was not long. It appeared to Michael that the soldiers who had been talking were sentries and that they might be circling the camp in opposite directions, making their rounds. Meeting again, the two men resumed their furtive conversation. Speaking in their native tongue (which Michael had learned well as a child), the soldiers expressed great disrespect for someone they called the madman.

"Isn't it enough that he murders his own sons because of his fear that they will steal his throne?" asked one.

"Not for him," remarked the second, deeper voiced soldier. "It's only a mystery that he hasn't done away with all of his heirs."

"I don't believe this Child we seek even exists, Octavian," said the first soldier.

"Oh, my good Sextus, in that, you are mistaken. He does live. And somehow we must see that this does not change."

"I don't understand."

"I have had the honor of serving under the great Zadoc, a man most highly regarded by Caesar. From his friends, the Wise Men of the East, Zadoc learned of the Savior born beneath the tail of that Star we saw a few years ago."

Michael's heart leapt at the mention of Zadoc, the Roman Tribune who had once helped him and his father escape the city where their lives had been in such danger.

"Could this man lead me to Zadoc, and Zadoc to my father?" Michael wondered. In the wake of that thought, his mind was filled with the old conflict between his desire to find his father and his duty to fulfill his mission. A deep sigh escaped him as he fought to gain control of his emotions.

"What was that?" Sextus asked.

"Nothing," Octavian said, disdain coloring his voice. "You're too jumpy. There's no one out here except our small force. One of the men is dreaming . . . that's all."

In the rushes, Michael held his breath, fear again washing over him as he thought of the consequences if he were found.

"We need to make our rounds again," Sextus said, and for a few minutes there was no sound except the small noises made by light sleeping horses and men.

When the sentries returned, Sextus took up the earlier conversation. "What does everything you told me earlier have to do with this Child we're trying to find?"

"I was coming to that when you were alarmed by someone's noisy breathing," Octavian said patiently. "The reason King Herod, the madman, wants this Child murdered is that he too has heard the Prophecy and he believes that this Boy was born to save the Jewish people and take over as their King."

"So why do you want to save the Boy? What's in it for you, Octavian?"

"Why must there always be a tangible reward? I have learned from Zadoc and others that great good can come to the world via this Child. I only hope to do my part to assure that the Boy lives long enough to fulfill His mission."

"What has all this to do with us, and with the Roman Empire we serve?"

"Our republic is dying an ugly death. Our leaders are corrupt. Even many of our soldiers have been bought off and lured into the debauchery of our fallen society. It is my hope that this Savior has come for all mankind, not just the Jews. In the light of this prospect, I will do my duty as I see it."

"But you speak treason, my friend," Sextus said almost gently.

"Treason against whom?" Octavian asked. "Caesar cares little or nothing for this mission on which he has sent us merely to quiet the demands of Herod."

"But Herod has immense power! Even our own centurion pays the madman obeisance, bowing and scraping before him as though he were a god!"

"Our centurion is the son of a Jewess and a Roman," Octavian reminded his companion. "As such, he deludes himself that Herod will one day elevate him to a position of power within his realm of authority."

"But you think this unlikely?" asked Sextus.

"I know it to be impossible," said Octavian firmly. "Herod has only disdain for this centurion and his fawning ways. The King may be mad, but he is no fool or simpleton. He recognizes duplicity in his underlings because in them, he sees himself."

"So, what if we find this Boy? What will you do?" Sextus asked.

"I wish I knew," Octavian answered and Michael could almost see him shaking his head. "I can only say that I will find a way to divert attention and enable Him and His family to escape."

"They *do* have fine horses," Sextus said with relish.

"What are you thinking?" asked Octavian angrily. "That we can bargain their lives against those of the horses?"

"Well . . ."

"Don't dare to consider such a thing. We don't even know for certain that they have these fabled horses. It was only a frightened shepherd . . . tortured in our absence by the vile centurion . . . who spoke of the young horseman and the horses."

The more Michael heard from the deep voiced Octavian, the more he wanted to meet the man. "There *are* good men," he thought, again recalling Zadoc with love and gratitude. "And they can sometimes be found in the most unlikely disguises."

"But how might the Family have escaped Herod's realm without such help and conveyance?" Sextus asked, drawing Michael back to the moment.

"Through stealth and cunning," Octavian answered. "These gifts are not reserved for the Roman army alone."

"But to have come such a great distance . . ." Sextus still sounded unconvinced.

"Stop this speculation!" the deep voice barked, then added more softly, "Sextus, you and I have been the friends of a lifetime, almost brothers after you lost your father and came to live with my family. I trust that you will keep this confidence and stand behind whatever I must do should we find this Child."

"You know that I honor you as my brother, your father as my own," Sextus replied with hurt in his tone. "How could you imagine that I might betray you?"

"It is only that there is so much at stake, and I have been remiss in sharing with you all that I have learned. When this march is over, we will take our holiday in Antioch where there are Wise Men who can educate you so that our understanding will be equal."

"Thank you, my brother. I will not disappoint you."

"I know this. Morning is near. We will talk again when it is safe. In the meantime, if we should encounter this Family as we continue our search for them, just follow my lead. I fear we might come across their camp in the next few days when we cross the river and explore again the area we passed by today."

"Octavian, there is something else I don't understand," Sextus said, a question in his voice. "Why have we been sent on this mission? We are not Herod's army. Caesar is our king."

"We have been sent on this fool's errand," Octavian answered contemptuously, "because Herod begged Caesar for our services. Sending us out in such small numbers, led by this centurion for whom he has so little respect~is

Caesar's way of placating Herod while at the same time voicing his lack of interest in the mission. Hasn't it occurred to you that throughout this journey we have traveled with less than one quarter of the common hundred man unit?"

"Yes . . ." Sextus hesitated. "But I just thought it was because of this centurion's disfavor . . . and I heard that he requested to lead this mission."

"That is true . . . but again, as I told you, our foolish leader thinks Herod will be grateful if he is responsible for the death of the Child, and that because he is half-Jewish, Herod will elevate him to a position of power within the Judean government."

His heart pounding as though he had been running for his life, Michael sneaked back to Lalaynia, swung onto her shining back, and let her take him quietly away from the encampment before she stretched out once more into the long gallop that would take them home.

This time, Michael paid attention to the journey, figuring the distance and the time it would take for the Roman soldiers to reach their home. As they had traveled toward the Star nearly seven years earlier, Lalaynia and her passenger covered ground at a most miraculous speed . . . crossing at least five times the area, Michael guessed, that the Romans could traverse in the same amount of time.

So, when they arrived at home just before dawn, Michael knew that the family had a few precious hours in which to determine their route and method of escape, and to make good that effort.

"Joseph," Michael called as Lalaynia slid to a stop in front of the cottage. "We are in grave danger! Please wake up! Please!"

"What happened?" Joseph asked, emerging at once through the doorway.

"The soldiers we glimpsed yesterday on the far horizon were sent by Herod in search of Jesus. They are camped only a few hours from here. We must make haste to escape them!"

"Perhaps they will continue traveling away from us," Joseph said.

"No! We need to find a place to hide!" Michael understood Joseph did not want to leave the home and business he had worked so hard to establish, but the horseman knew there was no other choice. "I heard them saying that in the next few days they will cross the river and explore this area again."

"But how do you know they seek Jesus?" Joseph asked.

Jesus came outside, rubbing still sleepy eyes with His small fists. Right behind Him was Mary, her face a mirror of fear. With everyone present, Michael quickly explained the events of the preceding hours, telling all that he had heard, including the story of the hapless shepherd.

"Our friend is right," said Mary when Michael finished speaking. "We must do as he says."

"We can't destroy all evidence of our home quickly enough," said Joseph reasonably. "If we abandon the place, the soldiers will simply continue their search in this area."

"What can we do?" asked Michael.

"You must take Jesus and the horses and escape into the hills," Joseph answered. "Mary and I will stay behind. If it is only the two of us they find, the soldiers will be thrown off the track. You said yourself, they seek a family with a young son, in the company of a horseman and his fine horses. These are the only clues they have as to our identity."

"I fear for your safety if we leave you behind. What if the shepherd gave them a description of our home place and its whereabouts?"

"I think this unlikely," responded Joseph. "After all, they have been traveling in the wrong direction. This would indicate that they do not know exactly where to look. But just in case the soldiers know they are looking for two dwellings, your tent can be quickly dismantled and packed onto the back of one of the horses. That way, only the house will remain. Come, you are right. We must not delay."

"But . . ." Though Michael wanted to protest, words failed him.

Calmer now, Mary reached up to touch Michael's cheek. "My dear friend," she said, "do not forget that we are protected by an army of God's angels. He will not forsake any of us. He has warned us of the danger so that we might be prepared. Now, we must again do His will."

"How will Jesus and I know when this threat has passed?"

"Only God has the answer to this question," Joseph said. "We must have faith in Him."

"Shall we return to this home?" Michael asked, still fearful of separation.

"I think not," answered Joseph. "Once the soldiers have departed, I think we must find a new home. This is no longer a safe place."

"How will we find each other?" Michael asked, a deep sorrow engulfing him as his heart recalled the losses of family he had already suffered.

"Trust God," Mary whispered. "He will show us the way."

Throughout this discourse, six-year-old Jesus had remained silent. Now he swung up onto the back of Zabbai. "Come, my brother," He said. "We need to hurry. We can come back to say good bye."

It took less then an hour for Michael and Jesus to dismantle and fold Michael's tent and to pack it carefully on

Esdraelon's broad back. By the time they returned to the house, Mary had packed provisions for many days and Joseph had filled several goatskins with water for the journey, all of which Michael added to Esdraelon's burden.

Joseph clasped the hands of Mary and Jesus, then beckoned Michael to join the circle. "Dear God," Joseph began, "we ask You to bless us and keep us while we are absent, one from the other. Provide safe passage for Jesus and Michael and bring us together again. Deliver us from fear. Give us the faith to know that You will send Your angels to protect us and to lead us back to one another in Your time."

"We are in My Father's hands," Jesus said. "All will be well."

Joseph bent down, picked Jesus up and held Him for long moments in his powerful embrace.

Mary reached for Michael's hand and looked into the young man's eyes. "I know that you will protect my Son and that God will protect you," she said. Then it was her turn to bid farewell to Jesus. When Joseph set the Boy back on His feet, Mary knelt so that their eyes could meet. She let her tears fall without shame, but she said nothing, only lost herself in the gaze of the precious Child God had given her.

Jesus caressed His mother's cheek with His small hand, comforting her and Himself in silence. Then He moved closer and wrapped His little arms around her neck. Joseph and Michael stood back, watching the mother and Son, silent tears overflowing their hearts and running down their bronzed cheeks. Finally, Jesus released His mother and she stood up. There was nothing more to be said as Michael and Jesus mounted their horses and rode away toward the hills and their uncertain future.

"Will you stay with us?" Rubria asked excitedly.

"Yes, I will stay," answered Archanus. "I am honored that your father has asked me to be your teacher . . ."

"And Luke's!" Rubria reminded. "You will like teaching him much better than me. He is very smart . . . and serious. I am just a happy girl . . . happier now that you have decided to stay."

"How could I do otherwise?" Archanus couldn't help but laugh with the child. "Your father opened his home to me when I was in need and allowed Keptah to spare no effort or expense for my healing."

"But you wanted to go in search of your son."

"One day, I will find Michael. But for now, I believe I have been called to remain here with you and Luke, to teach you all that I can and prepare you for this world."

"Will you tell us more about the Savior? The One who was born beneath the Star?"

"Yes, child, I will. But now you must go and leave me alone so that I can settle into my new quarters."

"And write another letter to your son?"

"Yes . . ."

"Why do you write to him when you don't know where to send these letters?"

"For the sake of hope." Archanus paused. "And so that even if I do not live to see him again, my heart might one day reach him through the thoughts I have written down."

"How will this be?"

"Perhaps you or Luke will meet him and give him these letters . . . and my love."

CHAPTER
Eight

CHAPTER Eight

wo days later, the Roman cadre arrived at the home of Mary and Joseph. Following Jesus and Michael's departure, the couple had prayed endlessly while they went about the tasks of dismantling Joseph's carpenter shop and carefully burying his tools in the enlarged garden where Mary grew their vegetables.

Joseph had raked away all evidence of the horses, mixing their leavings with the earth spread upon the new section of the garden. The few goats and the chickens for which they had long ago bartered browsed and scratched at the earth around the solitary house. Having seen the soldiers' approach, the couple had made themselves busy in the garden so that they appeared to be simple farmers, tending their land.

In single file, ten mounted soldiers approached, followed by an equal number of infantrymen. The lead horse pranced and tossed his head as the arrogant centurion who sat astride the animal alternately spurred him forward, then signaled him to stop with sharp yanks on the reins. The competing sounds of clanking armor, of forty shod hooves striking the ground in strange syncopation, of horses snorting and men marching demolished the peace of Mary and Joseph's home place.

At the edge of Mary's garden, the centurion jerked his giant black horse to a sharp halt, causing him to rear and strike at the air with his forelegs. Angrily, the horse cavorted, his front feet glancing off the ground before he whirled and reared again. All the while, in a display of dominance, his leering rider goaded on the fractious animal.

Mary moved almost imperceptibly closer to Joseph. Otherwise, the couple remained silent and seemingly composed. Had the soldier hoped that the man and wife would flee so that he and his fearsome mount could chase them down, he was disappointed. In silent prayer, the husband and wife remained stoical.

Finally, a second rider moved up beside the centurion and said gruffly, "We have come in search of a horseman and his mounts. What do you know of such a person."

"Why do you seek these, master?" asked Joseph.

"Octavian! Step aside!" ordered the centurion on the black horse. "I will handle this interrogation!"

Octavian stroked the mane of his fine golden stallion, dipped his chin in deference and backed the horse a step to signal his obedience.

"I am Carvilius," announced the centurion roughly. "Octavian and the others follow me in search of those suspected of treason. Where are your children, your servants?"

"We have no children and no servants," Joseph responded. "Nor do we know any horsemen."

"From where do you hail?" demanded the centurion. "Your skin has not the black cast of the Egyptian. Why are you here?"

"We are Jews," responded Joseph honestly. "Like many thousands of our race, we have chosen to settle in this land."

"And to escape your duty to pay taxes to Caesar?"

"No, sire. We pay our tax as do all of our countrymen."

"Have you proof?"

"Yes. Our annual receipt is inside our house."

"You will give us entrance to your home," Carvilius said in a sharp, condescending tone.

"You and your troops are welcome here," said Joseph. "I fear, however, that we do not have wine or provisions to serve all of you."

"We can care for ourselves," said the centurion. "You are under suspicion of harboring fugitives. We did not come to sample the pleasures of your household, merely to learn the truth and act accordingly." As he spoke, the man leveled a lascivious glare on Mary.

Again, Mary pressed closer to her husband, unable to hide her almost paralyzing fear. Joseph's arm trembled as he hugged his wife to him, and his heart raced with terror.

In response to Mary and Joseph's prayers, the angelic army that protected them had grown in number. In the face of the centurion's implied threat to Mary, the leader of the angels took charge, using Octavian to do his bidding.

"Carvilius," Octavian said sternly, "you are out of line! You will retreat and leave these people to me." Then, jumping down from his horse, Octavian took Joseph by the arm and turned him toward the cottage. "Come," the soldier said in a softer tone. "Bring your wife and show us through your house."

Behind the centurion, his troops snickered audibly, many nodding their heads as if in approval of Octavian's actions.

As his adopted brother entered the house with Mary and Joseph, Sextus urged his horse forward and engaged the centurion in conversation. "We must tend to the horses and set up camp for the night," he said.

At that, Carvilius jerked his black horse around in a hard turn and led the way to the bank of the river where he began shouting orders for the erection of a temporary encampment.

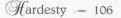

That night, Octavian and Sextus discussed the situation with a strangely subdued Carvilius.

"I do not trust their calm," said Carvilius. "They are hiding something. I can feel it."

"It is because of their faith that these people do not fear us," said Octavian. "They believe that their God will protect them."

"How do you know so much about the Jews?" Carvilius asked, suspicion coloring his tone.

"I am a student of their culture," answered Octavian, "as is the Tribune, Zadoc." Octavian dropped this powerful name knowing that the mention of the corrupt centurion's nemesis would frighten the man and remind him of Octavian's connection with Zadoc.

"If you know so much about these people, tell me, why are they really here?" Carvilius shifted his weight and brushed nervously at his tunic.

Octavian paused before answering, enjoying the centurion's discomfort. It had not been all that long ago since Zadoc warned Carvilius that he would suffer beyond his most hideous imagination, should any harm ever befall Octavian.

"It is as they have said," answered Octavian, his hard look meant to convey far more than his words. "Many thousands of their countrymen live in Egypt. This we know from the census and from our tax records. There is no mystery in this."

"Perhaps not," said Carvilius, his voice still betraying his agitation. "But this is a place that matches the shepherd's description."

"Only in part," offered Sextus. "Recall that the shepherd told us of two dwellings and three exceedingly fine horses, as well as a carpenter shop. Here is only one humble home and a meager garden."

"Still," whined the centurion, "I suspect deception. We will camp here until we have interrogated everyone who lives in this vicinity and the people in every settlement within a day's ride."

"But they have no mounts," Sextus reminded. "And there is only one small town within walking distance."

"Be still!" shouted Carvilius, running his hand through his hair and casting his gaze about as if looking for some sort of validation. "I will make these assessments without assistance from either of you. And I will please Herod by finding and doing away with the wretched Child! Now, leave me! I must rest."

"How did you do that?" Sextus asked Octavian when they were far enough away that the centurion could no longer hear their conversation.

"What?" asked Octavian innocently.

"You know what!" Sextus smiled and shook his head. "You've controlled the mad Carvilius all day."

Octavian placed a hand on his friend's shoulder and said quietly, "There are some things I neither understand, nor question. My words and my actions this day were not always my own. . . ."

❧

In the days that followed, Carvilius made good his threat to interrogate anyone who lived within what he considered a reasonable proximity. Members of the angelic army sent for Mary and Joseph's protection traveled with the soldiers, mysteriously erasing the memories of all those who were interrogated. Thanks to the angels, the centurion's efforts were thwarted at every encounter. Not one person questioned by the Romans could recall a child, a horseman or horses, nor did they know Joseph as anything but a poor farmer.

On the seventh day after their arrival, while Sextus directed the foot soldiers in the preparations for departure, the centurion, accompanied by Octavian, went to Mary and Joseph's house for one last attempt at catching the couple in a lie.

"When do you expect the others who live with you to return?" Carvilius asked.

Standing beside his horse, Octavian looked up at the mounted Carvilius and shook his head.

"There are no others, sire," said Joseph, his calm restored. "My wife and I live alone. Our God has not chosen to bless me with children of my loins."

Carvilius continued his badgering until, at last, Octavian interrupted, once again speaking with the authority of the angels. "We have spent enough time here. We must return to Judea for your audience with Herod and . . ." he paused deliberately, "for my meeting with Zadoc."

This time, Octavian mentioned Zadoc not only to intimidate the centurion, but also to pass a message to Mary and Joseph, whom he hoped might recognize the name. If, indeed, these people kept company with the young horseman, they would doubtless have heard the name Zadoc. And, if the rumors were true that the horseman was the son of Zadoc's dearest friend, Archanus, there was added reason to protect the peasants at all cost.

Carvilius scowled, then yanked back on the reins, pulling his black horse onto its hind legs. "Mark my words," he shouted down at Mary and Joseph, "if we do not find the Child, I will return . . . without Octavian! Be warned! It will not go so easily for you again!" At that he turned the big horse and spurred him into a hard gallop toward the river where his men awaited his command.

"You would do well to break camp," Octavian said softly to Mary and Joseph. "This place is no longer safe. Travel farther into the heart of this delta and lose yourselves for a time. It is rumored that Herod is not well. Once he is gone, the threat to the Child will diminish. Take heed, but be at peace."

❧

"God is good to have sent us a messenger in the guise of the soldier, Octavian," said Mary, taking Joseph's hand in her own.

"Yes, now, we must plan our departure," Joseph said. Then, thinking out loud, he added, "I wonder why the wicked Carvilius was unable to obtain information from our neighbors."

"We prayed for God's angels to protect us, my husband. We can only believe they came and delivered us from this threat. But now, I think you are correct. We must move with caution. It will take several weeks for this centurion to make his way to Jerusalem, meet with Herod and return."

"Indeed . . . and Octavian might cause the journey to take even longer."

After the soldiers departed, Joseph and Mary went to the home of Nathan and Lidah. The two couples, along with Nathan and Lidah's children, shared the evening meal. Afterwards, the boys went off to play, the men relaxed at the table, and the women went outside where they could share their own conversation.

"I'm afraid we must move on soon," Joseph said to Nathan as the two men sat sipping wine. "Perhaps you could help me sell some of our furniture. And maybe our animals and vegetables would be of use to your family."

"You will need beasts of burden," Nathan responded. "Why not make a trade?"

"That would be excellent," said Joseph, a quizzical frown creasing his forehead. "Do you not wish to know the reasons for our departure?"

"Do you wish to tell me?" asked Nathan.

"It would be difficult to explain. Perhaps one day . . ."

"I can obtain a donkey and a camel," Nathan went on without asking any questions. "If you will build one more of your fine tables and chairs to go with them, this, along with the goods and animals you leave behind will, be fair trade. Is this agreeable to you?"

"Yes," Joseph said with simple gratitude.

Outside, the women sat watching Lidah's sons at play.

"They are fine boys," said Mary, her heart aching for Jesus.

"Yes," said Lidah. "They are a great joy to me." Then, reaching over to pat her friend's arm, she added, "Don't despair, Mary. One day you'll have fine sons of your own."

Realizing that the angels had permanently removed this family's memory of Jesus and Michael, Mary said only, "I will miss you, my friend."

"We will meet again," said Lidah, tears escaping her dark eyes. "Of this I am sure. We are friends of the heart. And we will meet again."

Preparing for their journey, Joseph worked long hours building goods which he would trade, along with the goats, the chickens, and succulent vegetables from Mary's garden, for a camel and a donkey. On the night before they were to leave, Nathan arrived at their home with the animals he had promised to provide and a wagon in which he would carry away his goods.

"Lidah could not come along," he said when Mary stepped out of her house. "Little Marcus has had a bad fever and she did not want to leave him."

"I understand," said Mary, tears filling her eyes as they had so often lately.

"We will see one another again," Nathan said. "Lidah is sure of this, and she is rarely mistaken."

After the wagon was loaded, Nathan left and with Mary's help Joseph made final preparations.

The next morning, in front of their house for the last time, Joseph took Mary's hands in his, looked up at the open sky and prayed. "You have kept us safe these many years, through every kind of peril. We can only believe that You have also protected Michael and Jesus during their absence from us. We ask now that You would lead us to these ones we love."

Traveling west, away from the rising sun, the husband and wife were silent. Neither looked back at the home they left behind but kept their eyes on the soft light that embellished the morning sky ahead. Each used hope as a weapon against the fear that sought to destroy them.

"Michael!" Archanus called out, awakening himself from a dream so real that he could not, at first, remember where he was. Arising slowly from his bed, he pressed a shaking hand to his head. His body ached. The scars from the wounds made by the robbers' swords throbbed without mercy. Straining to make out his surroundings, he felt trapped in the darkness, alone and afraid. Fleetingly, he wondered if he had fallen back into the sleep of near death where he had once lingered for so long.

"Are you alright?" Luke spoke from the doorway, his voice filled with concern.

"I . . . I don't know . . ." Still disoriented, Archanus struggled toward reality.

"You must have been dreaming," Luke offered. "I heard you from my room. You were calling out for Michael, bidding him to take care."

"The dream," Archanus whispered, recalling . . .

They were galloping across a great plain, he and Michael. And there was a small boy with them, riding a glorious gray stallion. Soldiers in clanking armor were close behind, shouting threats and warnings. Then they were charging down a steep hill into a ravine and robbers pursued them, not soldiers. Archanus was turning to face the assailants, to keep them from following Michael and the little boy . . .

"Archanus." Luke placed a strong hand on the older man's shoulder. "It's alright. It was only a dream."

Finally, back in the moment, Archanus shuddered and shook his head as if to clear his mind. "The dream . . . it was so real. But, I wonder, who was the boy?"

"Your son?" Luke asked.

"No, there was another. My son was a man grown . . . but there was a little boy with him on a magnificent gray horse." He paused. "Luke, they're in danger. I can feel it."

"Archanus, you have told me how you and your son used to communicate without words. Could this be happening now? Could he be calling to you from far away?"

"I don't know." Archanus ran his hand through his thick, still dark hair. "I don't know where he could be, or who could be with him. I don't know how I can help him now." Despair colored his tone.

"You must pray. . . . and hope, as you and Keptah have taught me to do. You must believe that the One God remains with your son."

CHAPTER *Nine*

O n the day of their departure, a deep silence hung between Michael and Jesus. Constantly alert for danger, Michael searched his heart for the faith he knew he must have on this journey. He wondered what could be going through the mind of his young companion, but he didn't ask, recalling how difficult it had been to share his own feelings under similar circumstances.

As they traveled, Michael settled into the familiar habit of giving Lalaynia her head and allowing her to chart the course. Losing track of time, much as he had on his first mysterious pilgrimage more than six years earlier, Michael thought about the differences between this assignment and the previous one.

"At least this time," he thought, "I know that my mission is to protect Jesus. And even though I don't know where we're going, I've learned to trust Lalaynia to lead the way. It's still hard not to be afraid. But I've seen how the angels can protect us, so the fear isn't nearly as awful as it once was."

But this time, there were other mysteries. Where would they find a safe place to stay? Would they ever be reunited with Mary and Joseph? Or would Jesus be deprived of His parents as Michael had been?

"How can I know?" Michael whispered, reaching down to stroke Lalaynia's neck. "And not knowing, how can I pretend, so that Jesus doesn't sense my concern?"

Forcing himself to abandon this train of thought, Michael turned his attention to the horses that had always been his greatest comfort. Lalaynia had one of those ground-covering walks that every horseman loves. Her head bobbing in rhythm with her steps, she had to lengthen her stride even further than normal to stay ahead of her longer-legged son. Esdraelon, carrying the travelers' supplies, had to jog to keep up. Happiness lit Michael's face as he allowed himself to feel the power, the determination and the confidence of the sweet mare as she carried him again into the unknown.

"Do the horses hope?" he wondered. "Do they feel all of our emotions as they feel our fear?"

"The animals understand us. They feel what we feel," Jesus said, riding up beside Michael, answering the silent question and making the horseman wonder if he had spoken out loud.

"Are you tired?" Michael asked, taken by surprise at Jesus' words and unable to think quickly what else to say.

"No," Jesus answered, "I'm fine . . . and in My heart there is enough hope for us both."

❧

They camped the first night on a tiny islet hidden deep in the rushes beside the Nile. They cared for the horses first, then sat down to share some of the provisions that Mary had sent. Worried by the sadness that had settled over Jesus, Michael asked the Boy if He was all right.

"I don't mean to be a burden," Jesus said, "and I am still hopeful. It's just that I miss My mother and father . . ."

Michael moved closer to his young charge and put an arm around Him, attempting to console without the words that he knew would give away his own uncertainty.

Jesus rested His head on Michael's chest, silent tears making tracks down His cheeks until sleep overtook Him. Michael sat upright throughout the night, holding Jesus in his arms, occasionally leaning back against the foreleg of Zabbai who stood right behind him until dawn. Shadow curled up against Jesus, offering his own brand of comfort to the Boy he loved beyond all others.

Through the long watches of the night, Michael recalled how his father had once sat awake, guarding him as he slept. He watched the half moon make its way across the blue-black sky. His anxiety over the future fought with the memories of his past, until at last he thought to pray . . . to ask for help, for wisdom, for protection.

"Will I now be the earthly father to this Boy?" he asked. "Dear God, how can I ever be equal to the task You have set before me?"

Finally, the night passed. The stars dimmed, then retreated into the wakening sky. With the dawn, Michael's fears stepped back, and in their place, tentative stirrings of hope lit his spirit like the sun whispering its intent to rise.

Jesus awoke to the songs of morning birds, the snorts of the horses, and the sound of Michael humming a soft tune. Rubbing sleep from His eyes in the little Boy gesture that Michael had come to love, Jesus smiled at His protector. "Thank you, My brother," He said, His face a mirror of the peace that was more commonly His.

Michael leaned his head back and stretched his neck, then stood up, grateful to work out the stiffness that came from sitting too still through the night. "Are You feeling better today?" he asked with the compassion of one who has experienced similar pain.

"Yes . . . My Father came to me last night in a dream. He has promised that we will be safe . . . and that we will be reunited with the ones we love."

Michael smiled, surprised again by the sense of peace that Jesus could impart with just a few words.

✻

For many days, Lalaynia chose the route of travel with her customary calm assurance, crossing arms of the Nile where the water was low and narrow. Michael wondered if she found her way by uncanny instinct, or Divine guidance, until finally he realized that the "why" of it didn't really matter. Either way, it was a gift from the One God.

On the seventh day, Lalaynia headed into a narrow canyon that appeared at first to have no exit. Soon, however, she began climbing up out of the ravine, creating a switchback path toward a summit beyond the riders' range of vision. For several hours they climbed the steep, often treacherous path. When they at last broke over the ridge, Michael and Jesus were met with a dazzling sight.

Before them spread a broad, high meadow with flora and fauna of the type Michael had not seen since he traveled the far northern mountains with the horsemen. Sparkling springs dotted the meadow making clear pools around which berry bushes and fruit and nut trees flourished. Lush grasses grew everywhere, in some places belly deep to the tallest horse. Sweet clover and succulent short grasses spread out from the springs. The honeyed sound of songbirds filled the pine scented air.

A coniferous forest rimmed the meadow and climbed the hills that surrounded the basin. "It is paradise!" Michael exclaimed, jumping down from Lalaynia's back to savor the cool waters of a spring.

"It is!" Jesus exclaimed, as a brilliant bluebird lit upon Zabbai's long neck, looking into the eyes of the Boy as if resuming a conversation. "Lalaynia has brought us to a more beautiful home than we could have imagined."

At the edge of the forest, Michael and Jesus established camp, then set about the business of waiting. Jesus seemed to take it for granted that one day soon Mary and Joseph would appear. But Michael remained apprehensive, usually sleeping fitfully . . . until one moonless night when he fell into a deep sleep.

On that occasion, Michael's special angel came to give him much needed comfort. "You must hold fast to hope," the angel said. "Without it you live in a void. God is with you and with His Son. He wants you both to be filled with joy. He has blessed you with this time together, and He does not want the gift to be made less by your fears or old sorrows."

When Michael awoke the next morning, he looked to the mat where Jesus slept, wishing to share with the Boy his renewed peace. But Jesus had already gotten up and was standing nearby, absently stroking Shadow's soft head and watching Michael.

"I prayed for you last night, My brother," Jesus said, and at once, Michael understood. He no longer questioned the ways nor the wisdom of this Child, merely accepted and was thankful.

Days passed with the young man and the Boy, aboard Esdraelon and Zabbai, exploring the forest and the mountains that encircled their home. Jesus frolicked in the meadow with all manner of woodland creatures, most of which He had never known before. The companions feasted on the fruits and nuts and berries that grew in wild profusion wherever there was a spring. It was, as the angel had said, a time for these brothers of the heart to deepen and strengthen the bond that would remain unmatched by any friends, any brothers, throughout the ages.

Having promised Mary and Joseph that Jesus' education would not be neglected in their absence, Michael brought out Joseph's treasured scrolls each day and sat with Jesus while the Boy read. They worked sums together and Jesus practiced each of the languages that Michael knew. The Boy quickly mastered the Hebrew's Aramaic, as well as the Romans' language, and the Greek that Michael favored.

But Jesus was like any boy; He needed exercise and a time to play. Understanding this, Michael taught Jesus many of the games he had seen the children of his mother's people enjoy. So it was that as a young man, Michael at last learned to play like a child.

Soon Jesus began drawing Zabbai and Esdraelon into the games. At first, He taught them to play tag while He and Michael remained on the ground. Then He invented riding challenges. Before long they were enjoying daily races with Michael aboard Esdraelon and Jesus on Zabbai.

In truth, there was no contest, so superior was Zabbai's athleticism. So the races became a wonderful excuse to let the horses stretch out and run like the wind. All the while, Lalaynia, now an old mare, stood watching like a proud, if censorious, mother, too dignified to be involved with childish diversion. Because there was no way he could keep up with the horses, Shadow remained with Lalaynia, barking and leaping happily in the air each time the riders returned.

One day, just when Michael had decided it was time to teach Jesus how to stand up on a horse's back, Zabbai came galloping across the meadow with Jesus in a full standing position, arms out-flung, head thrown back, His laughter ringing in the wind.

Sometimes in the afternoons when Michael was rubbing down the horses after a day of strenuous exercise, Jesus and Shadow would sit near their favorite spring and wait for the forest creatures to join them. The first visitor was almost always the curious raccoon, followed by rabbits and birds, deer and foxes. Sometimes a bear or an elk would even appear. With His little friends gathered around Him, Jesus would begin to speak, telling stories that held the animals deep in His thrall.

On one of their forays into the forest, Zabbai led the way to a new lookout, a promontory high above the Nile River valley. The delta spread before them for as far as the eye could see, and from here, Jesus and Michael could observe all that went on below.

It became their regular daily custom to ascend to this vantage point. Though neither spoke of their mission, it was tacitly understood that they were watching and hoping for signs of Mary and Joseph. They knew not how the couple would find their way; they simply trusted that it would happen.

Twenty-two days after their initial departure, Jesus' and Michael's faith was rewarded. When they arrived at their lookout late in the afternoon, they saw below a woman aboard a donkey with a man at her side leading a heavily laden camel.

"Could it be Your parents?" Michael wondered aloud.

"It is!" Shouting joyfully, Jesus jumped up from His place on the rock and fairly flew onto Zabbai's back.

"Wait!" Michael couldn't help but join Jesus in His eagerness. "I'm excited too . . . but we have to wait until nightfall."

"Why can't we go now?"

"Because we can't take any chances," Michael said patiently. "We need to stay here until we're certain they haven't been followed. Then, under the cover of darkness, we'll go to their camp. Once we're sure of their identity, we'll make ourselves known and bring them to our new home."

Jesus fidgeted all afternoon, climbing on and off of Zabbai, jogging out into the meadow, tossing small stones down the hill. All the while, Michael sat watching the day wane, willing himself to remain patient. The valley below turned tawny as the sun began its descent behind the forest. Gradually the mountain shadows spread across the delta, cooling the fecund earth. The man unpacked his camel and erected a small tent beside the river while the woman made a fire and prepared the evening meal. Behind Jesus and Michael, the horses grazed patiently as if they understood they must rest for the night's mission.

"Can we go now?" Jesus asked when the shadows of evening had devoured the light.

"Yes." Michael grinned and ruffled Jesus' hair affectionately. "We'll go get Lalaynia so she can carry Your mother. By the time we leave our high meadow, the full moon will have begun its ascent so that we'll be able to see the way more clearly."

Four hours later, they stopped beside the river near the camp. "Stay with the horses," Michael said to Jesus. "Let me be sure it's truly Mary and Joseph before we make ourselves known. We still can't be too careful."

As Michael approached, he heard the man and the woman talking softly.

"Where can they be?" Mary asked, her distress and exhaustion obvious. "We have traveled nearly the entire breadth of the delta with no sign or word of them."

"Don't forget the angels," Joseph responded. "We have not traveled aimlessly, nor has our journey been in vain. God's angels are our guides, and they will lead us to reunion."

"I am sorry, dear husband. My faith is greater than my words. It is just that I am tired and I miss my Son so . . ."

"You will miss Him no longer," said Michael, his voice alive with joy as he entered the camp.

Mary and Joseph jumped at once to their feet and ran to embrace Michael. "But where is Jesus?" Mary asked anxiously.

"I am here!" shouted Jesus.

Joseph bent over and scooped Jesus up, embraced the Boy in a powerful hug, then reached for Mary and drew her into the circle of his arms.

Everyone talked at once, hardly able to contain their excitement, until finally Michael brought calm to the moment.

"We need to break camp here and make our way up the mountain," he said. "The camel and the donkey will slow us down, and we don't want to be seen by anyone."

Soon Mary was mounted on Lalaynia, the couples' belongings were distributed between the camel and the donkey, and Joseph rode behind Jesus on Zabbai. Lalaynia allowed Esdraelon to lead the way until it came time to climb up out of the canyon. Then, as she had done when she first brought Jesus and Michael to this place, she picked a careful course.

Though day had broken by the time they arrived in the meadow, Mary insisted that everyone rest. "You can show us

everything when the sun begins to warm this high place," she assured her Son. "Until then, let's sleep a while so that we will be fresh for our explorations."

"It is indeed a paradise," said Joseph the next day when the Family had completed a tour of the broad meadow. "God has brought us to a perfect land where we can rest and await His call. How dearly He must love us. But I have never seen anything like this . . . the landscape . . . the animals?"

"My father once told me of animals like these who live in other lands far away," offered Michael. "And in the north there are mountains . . . but none quite like these."

"My Father has created this magical place and its creatures especially for us," said Jesus mysteriously.

Even in this moment of peace, Michael wondered. Always, he had learned, there was calm before the storm. And never in his life had any sweetness lasted long enough. He could not forget the peril they had all so recently escaped, nor could he quell the fear that evil would find them again and steal their safety . . . just as evil seemed to have stolen everything else he had ever truly loved.

⌒ MEANWHILE NEAR ANTIOCH ⌒

"I fear that Archanus regrets his decision to remain with us," Luke said to Keptah while the two worked together one afternoon.

Keptah did not respond at once, but seemed to be contemplating his answer. Finally, he said, "I don't think this is the case. You are sensitive to him, and this is good. But you must not take responsibility for what he is feeling."

"I know he pines for his son. I know I have done nothing to displease him. I just think he feels trapped by his gratitude and his sense of honor."

"Have you spoken to him of this?"

"Well . . . in a way. I told him he mustn't stay on my account."

"And what about Rubria," Keptah asked. "Has she no say in this?"

"Rubria is a child who does not understand . . ."

"And you are a man who does?" Keptah interrupted.

"You know what I mean," Luke said, embarrassed. "Rubria's small world revolves around her. When she asks for a prize, her father cannot wait to provide it."

"Do you think she sees Archanus as a prize?"

"NO! Not at all. She loves Archanus. How do you twist me in such knots? And why?"

"I want you to think everything through. I do not mean to confuse you but to clarify."

"I beg you to do so." Luke sighed. "Please, tell me how Archanus feels since he won't share his emotions with me. I only want him to be happy."

Again, Keptah paused. "He loves both you and Rubria as though you were his own. He does feel a debt of gratitude to Rubria's father. But he does not feel trapped. Of all of this, he has assured me."

"Then what is it?"

"Because of your deep caring, I think that Archanus would agree that you should understand his reasons for remaining here. He has told you of the angel who has visited him in the past, has he not?"

"Yes . . ."

"Not long ago, that angel returned and told Archanus that the One God wishes for him to remain with you."

"But why? And why has he not told me this?"

"The reason was not revealed to him, only the mission. And he has not told you because he didn't want you to feel guilty. Be at peace, Luke, this is God's will."

CHAPTER
Ten

CHAPTER Ten

Where the woodland met the eastern rim of the meadow, Joseph chose a place to build a house. "We can use dead trees from this fine forest," he explained to Michael as they planned the project.

"I'll bring you the best of the standing dead and recently fallen trees," Michael said, excited to start working.

"Me too!" Jesus piped up. "I want to help too!"

"You're too small to be cutting down trees." Mary smiled at her Son. "You can help me . . ."

"I have an idea," Michael interrupted, understanding how Jesus felt. It had never been fun, he recalled, to be treated like he was too little or too young to be of help. "We'll make a litter like my Mother's people use to pull things behind the horses. I'll cut the trees and lay them on the litter. We can use Esdraelon as the workhorse. and Jesus can ride him from the forest where I'm cutting the trees to the building site and back."

"Yes!" laughed Jesus. "Esdraelon and I will be the wood carriers."

When Mary gave Michael an agreeable glance, he knew she approved of his plan.

"A great idea," Joseph added. "Let's get started."

In short order, Michael fashioned a harness and litter for Esdraelon. Then, accompanied by Joseph, he and Jesus rode the gelding into the forest where they began picking out the trees that looked best for the job. Joseph marked his first choices with a chalky substance. Michael cut these with one of Joseph's saws and placed them on the litter.

"Just look for others like these," Joseph said as he and Jesus left to go back to the edge of the meadow where the carpenter would begin his task.

Michael watched as the father and Son rode away. Sometimes his heart still ached so fiercely for his own father that he could scarcely bear the pain. But after a while, willing himself to close that particular door of his mind, he returned to the work at hand.

"I'm back!" called Jesus happily when He returned some time later for the next load.

"Good! I'm ready for you . . ."

"I'll help you put the trees on the litter," said Jesus, jumping down from the back of Esdraelon and trotting over to the trees that Michael had stacked. While the powerful young horseman easily lifted a fairly large tree, Jesus began to tug at the end of a smaller one. Not wanting to embarrass the Boy, Michael choked back a laugh when Jesus, unable to budge the heavy tree, lost His grip and fell back onto His small behind.

"It's all right," Michael said, still struggling not to chuckle. "This is a man's job. These trees, you know, are a lot bigger than You are!"

"But I want to help you . . ."

Michael reached down to pull Jesus to His feet and was caught off guard by the quick and obvious change in the Boy's mood. A faraway look in His eyes, Jesus said enigmatically, "Yes, the tree IS heavy . . . but in this life there will be far greater burdens."

As though he had crossed into a place where there was only darkness, Michael became consumed by dread. His heart in his throat, the horseman dropped to one knee beside Jesus and looked beseechingly into the eyes of the Child . . . eyes that seemed at once the gateway to all that had been and all that would one day be.

"I'm sorry I made you sad," Jesus whispered, reaching out His small hand to caress the cheek of the man who knelt before Him. "One day, My brother . . . one day, we will understand everything. Until then, we must both remember that with My Father's help, no burden is too great, and nothing is impossible."

⁂

For several days, Michael and Jesus continued gathering trees while Joseph stripped their bark then carefully placed and anchored them making the walls of the new house. When he had finished with the exterior walls and roof, he put up a dividing wall, creating a room for Michael and Jesus to share. Summer was nearly gone. The golden days of approaching autumn were shorter, and the nights were turning cold. Though Jesus and Michael protested, Mary wished for them to live in the house, rather than to camp outdoors. She even insisted that her husband erect a covered haven for the horses in case of inclement weather.

The days passed quickly with everyone joining in the construction of the new settlement. Engrossed in his work,

Michael didn't notice that Lalaynia was not herself. For many months, even before they left the delta, the old mare had stayed close to home. She had adopted this habit so gradually in the old home place that it never really appeared as a change.

Here, from the beginning, the mare seemed content to spend her days grazing peacefully in the company of the small woodland creatures even when Jesus and Michael rode off on one of their explorations aboard Zabbai and Esdraelon. So when Lalaynia began remaining most of the time near Mary and not eating well, only the young mother saw the change.

One morning after the house and the workshop had been completed and insulated against the gathering chill, Michael awoke earlier even than usual. In front of the houses, Zabbai stood nickering and softly pawing at the ground. "What is it?" Michael asked, fear gripping his heart. "Have the Romans found us?" Zabbai tossed his head and nickered again, then turned and began to jog toward the center of the meadow. Following at once, Michael could see Esdraelon standing near the main spring, but there was no sign of Lalaynia. Unwanted awareness and desperate sorrow overtook him even before he arrived and found Lalaynia lying deathly still in the field of clover she loved, surrounded by all of the birds and small animals that had become her companions.

"No," Michael cried out, instantly understanding that Lalaynia was dying. "It can't be your time. You can't leave me. Oh why have I not seen that you were failing? How could I not have known?"

Michael fell to his knees beside the dying mare. His tears overflowed and his powerful chest heaved with deep sobs. Moving closer, he sat down and lifted Lalaynia's head, then placed it gently in his lap. Stroking her beautiful mane as he had done a thousand times over the years, he began to sing a soft song, an unbidden melody that had lingered in his heart since a time beyond memory. Lost in blessed remembrance, he was transported from this meadow and his present grief. The days of his life with Lalaynia and the times he had known before her drifted across his heart and filled his spirit.

He saw his beautiful mother, her golden hair awash with wind and sunlight, as she galloped across a field aboard the fine gelding, Eleuzis. He heard his father's voice, telling the stories of the Magi. He saw the magnificent herd into which Lalaynia had been born, and recalled how she had chosen him when he sought a mount for the mission which took them both from that herd. He felt the wind in his face as it had been on the miraculous ride toward the Star.

As if sharing that ride with her boy once more, Lalaynia stirred, her nostrils flared, and her great heart surged once more.

"Don't go, old girl." Michael's words caught in a sob. "Please don't leave me. I cannot bear to lose you too. You are all that has been constant in my life, all that connects me to those we both once knew."

The pain in Michael's heart overpowered the reason in his mind. He could not think, but only feel, and for a time his grief became his only reality. Then all at once he felt the gentle touch of a hand on his shoulder and he turned to see Mary standing beside him.

"You must let her go," Mary whispered. "It is her time. She has served us all so very well. Now she must leave us."

"Why didn't I see this coming," Michael sobbed, letting his head fall against Mary. "How could I have been so callous and unfeeling? I should have felt her pain, seen her decline."

"I don't think she had any pain. And her decline was gentle. She has not suffered, nor must you."

Still gripped by emotion, Michael could say no more. Nor did Mary speak or move again. Awaiting the birth of the sun, the eastern sky warmed, but the birds of morning sang no welcoming song. Long moments of stillness were at last broken by the sound of running footsteps.

Understanding dawned on Jesus as it had on Michael, and for the first time the joyful and vigorous Boy was faced with death. Wordlessly, Jesus fell to the ground and wrapped His arms around Lalaynia's neck. Kneeling beside her Son, Mary stroked His head with one hand and the mare's face with the other.

"You are the mother of Zabbai," Jesus sobbed. "You cannot leave him. We cannot be without our mothers . . . Please . . . please don't go."

Tears overflowed and ran down Mary's cheeks. Her lips moved in silent prayer as she continued to stroke her Son's fair head and the mare's face.

Soon, Joseph appeared. Michael raised his eyes, gaining comfort from his friend's presence. Exhaling a deep breath, he placed a hand on Jesus' shoulder and echoed Mary's words, "We have to let her go," he said softly. "Her time has come."

Jesus looked up, His bright and shining eyes imploring. "Why can't I save her?" He cried to the heavens. "Why have I no power to bring her back? She is all that is left to Michael of his yesterdays. Why can I not give him the gift of her dear life?"

Though tears glistened on Mary's cheeks, her voice was clear and strong. "My Son, it is not Your Father's will. Lalaynia has given her life in His service. Now it's time for her to return home to Him."

"But what about Michael?" Jesus implored. "Without Lalaynia he has nothing left of his old life."

"He has his memories . . . and he has our love," Mary said, touching her Son's cheek. "Your Father will not forget what this good man has done . . . and Michael will never be alone."

The tall grass swayed and the trees sang as a strong breeze crossed the land. A bank of clouds that had hovered just above the horizon climbed higher, and from beneath them brilliant rays fanned out like the hand of God reaching down to touch the earth. A softer light fell across Michael's face, warming him, embracing his spirit. He lifted Jesus' chin and looked at the Boy with love and compassion.

"I'm ready to let her go," Michael said. "Your Father has spoken to my heart. I know that I must release this gentle spirit into His everlasting care."

"But will you not miss her?" Jesus asked.

"Only for a while," Michael stood up and moved closer to Zabbai. "For the first time ever, I understand that those who pass from this life into the next are the ones who are most blessed."

Thinking then about the road ahead and the one behind, Michael looked off across the valley to the mountains in the distance. Finally, he spoke again. "We grieve for our own loss, for the separation, for our loneliness. But I know now that when our journeys are over, we will join my Mother and Lalaynia and Ghadar, and we'll never be lonely again . . ."

"Michael is right," said Mary. "All those we have loved on this earth, we will meet again in heaven."

"To know this," added Joseph, "is to accept the peace God offers."

At that, Lalaynia took one last, long breath, and then she was gone.

And Jesus wept.

A deep stillness settled over the gathering. Michael knelt beside Lalaynia, stroking her neck, his heart reaching out to her across the silence, as though she could still feel the love he offered. Mary put her arms around Jesus and held Him to her. Joseph stood beside his wife, a welcome support.

"Come," Mary said after a time. "We need to prepare a resting place for our old friend."

Joseph took charge, and when the burial was completed, he led his family in prayer.

"Through this dear creature," Joseph said, "You have blessed the world for all time. You chose Lalaynia to rescue Your Son from the evil that threatened to take Him from us. And through her, You gave us Zabbai . . ."

As if understanding that Joseph spoke of him, Zabbai stepped forward and nuzzled Jesus softly. The Boy reached up and stroked the stallion's face, then turned His eyes to the sky. "Thank You, Father . . ." He bit His lip and choked back a sob. "Thank You for Lalaynia. I loved her so much and I know I'll see her again," He whispered, wiping at His tears, "but it's so hard to say good bye."

Michael moved closer, placed one hand on Zabbai's withers and rested the other on the Boy's shoulder. "I believe Your Father has spoken to my heart this morning . . ."

Zabbai reached around just then and bumped his soft nose at Jesus as if telling Him to listen.

"What did He tell you?" Jesus asked.

"He has given me to understand that from this day forward, He will use the great horses that descend from Zabbai to connect all the peoples of His vast creation."

Again, the stallion nuzzled Jesus' face. "Zabbai understands." Jesus smiled for the first time since Lalaynia's passing.

"I think You're right," Michael said, returning the Boy's look of joy. "I think Zabbai knows that the horses that carry his blood down through the ages will be the noblest of all." The horseman ran his hand along Zabbai's back. "And I think he knows that through these horses the One God will alter the course of history."

"And Lalaynia," added Mary, "will really never die . . ."

"How can this be?" asked Jesus.

"Wherever there are fine horses and true horsemen," Michael answered for Mary, "Zabbai's legacy will be known. And through that legacy, Lalaynia will live on."

With the back of His small hand, Jesus wiped away the last vestiges of His tears. "If Lalaynia were here," he said, "she would take us on an adventure. I think Zabbai will be the leader now."

At this, Joseph bent down and picked Jesus up, enfolded the Boy in a powerful hug, then lifted Him onto Zabbai's back.

Turning toward the mountains in response to the light pressure of Jesus' leg against his side, Zabbai took off at an easy lope. Mary and Joseph and Michael watched as the horse and rider moved away. They saw Jesus riding high, His head flung back, His arms outstretched in salutation. They saw Him bend forward to wrap His arms around Zabbai's neck and bury His face in the stallion's mane. And, left behind, they felt the Wind of the Spirit as it passed by, sweeping across the land to join Jesus on His journey toward destiny.

MEANWHILE NEAR ANTIOCH

Near the home of the Tribune, Diodorus, Archanus stood gazing out across a field of horses. Huge thunderheads burst into the southern sky. A warm wind drifted over the backs of the resting animals, and the Wise Man was taken back to a time he would never know again. "Oh, my son," he whispered, "I wonder if the horses were able to heal you . . . to carry you beyond your sadness . . . to help you forget, and to remember?"

"They are powerful creatures . . . and beautiful," Keptah said as he approached his friend, pretending not to have heard Archanus' plaintive words.

"Symbols of freedom," said Archanus

"Do you feel bound?" Keptah asked.

"Only by my longing . . ."

"It is not over . . . your life."

"I know . . . and my hope is not gone . . . It is only hiding for a while, somewhere beyond the mountains."

"Your wounds have healed and you are growing stronger by the day." Keptah paused.

"One day soon I must leave the safety of this fine house and go in search of my son."

"When that time comes, you will not travel alone."

CHAPTER
Eleven

CHAPTER *Eleven*

Dust motes danced on the ray of sunlight that broke through the open window. The chuf-chuf rhythm of a saw moving smoothly through a piece of wood was punctuated by the tap-tap of a small hammer. The hardy odor of cedar mingled with the aromas of less pungent woods, bringing life to the air in the carpenter's shop. From the doorway, Michael watched, and listened, and delighted in the scene before him.

Kneeling in a pool of light where the sun ray struck the floor, eight-year-old Jesus concentrated on the effort of making a little wooden box. His lower lip clamped between His teeth, His eyes focused on His target, a choke hold on His child-sized hammer, Jesus carefully aimed every stroke toward the nails that relentlessly eluded Him.

Nearby, Joseph stood cutting short logs that would eventually be the legs of a chair. On the wall, the tools of Joseph's woodworking and masonry trades were hung with the same care and precision the man gave to his work. In the corner of the room a small pile of sawdust sat beside the broom that, over the course of the workday, would periodically be used to keep the floor tidy.

"Ouch!" Jesus cried out, breaking the subtle cadence of the place and the moment.

Michael smiled, thinking of the many small mishaps he had suffered when Joseph began teaching him to use a hammer. But when Jesus held His hand up toward Joseph and Michael saw that there was blood running down the Boy's suntanned arm and real tears flowing from His eyes, Michael rushed at once to summon Mary for help.

"It's all right," Joseph was saying soothingly, when Michael returned to the shop with Mary. "We'll clean the wound and wrap it. It will be all right."

Kneeling beside her Son, Mary brushed back a lock of hair from His dirty forehead and placed a kiss there. Taking His wounded hand tenderly in her own, she dipped a cloth in the basin of clean water that Michael had brought from the house and cleansed the wound. "How did You do this, My Son?" she asked.

"I . . . I . . . I . . . tried . . ." Jesus stuttered through small, silent sobs.

"It's all right," Joseph said again, running his big hand across the Boy's head.

"He was making a box for you." Joseph said to Mary. "He was learning to nail the pieces together. I think the nails kept escaping, so He must have been holding one too close to the point. When He hit it with the hammer, it went through His finger before it went into the wood."

"Ye . .Ye . . . Yes . . . I . . . hit it . . ." Jesus still struggled to choke back His tears and explain.

Mary calmed her Son with slow, patient ministrations and gentle words. When the salve and bandage was applied, she leaned back, making ready to stand. A ray of sunlight filled the place where she had been and embraced the child in its brilliance. A hush fell over the room until, lifting His eyes to the light, Jesus whispered, "But He was pierced for our transgressions . . . and by His wounds we were healed."

"What did You say?" Michael asked, confused by a vague recollection.

"Those were the words of our prophet Isaiah when he spoke of the Savior," Joseph explained, anguish dominating his voice and his features.

"But what did You mean?" Michael asked, turning again to Jesus.

"I don't really know," Jesus answered, shaking His head. "Sometimes in the light, My Father speaks to Me. But I don't always understand."

An uneasy quiet took hold of the companions as each tried to find some message in the words Jesus had spoken. Finally, Michael suggested that he and Jesus take the horses and go exploring. Joseph returned to his labors, and Mary walked out into the meadow to think about the gift, and the great trust, she had received from her God.

Drawn, as she often was, to the spring where Lalaynia had spent her last days, Mary sat down in the clover beside the glistening pond. Relishing the warmth of the sun, she allowed herself to be lost for a time in the miracle and the mystery that had become her very essence. Like a feather in the wind, the young mother drifted on the current of memory until she found her way back to the day and the time when it all began . . .

The afternoon was hot and still. Pungent odors mingled, creating for the town a piquant scent all its own. There were strident sounds of merchants hawking their wares, women calling to one another and scolding their children, a blacksmith plying his trade, the rolling wheels of a trader's wagon, and birds conversing busily on the rooftops.

From the heart of this common scene, a girl's clear spirit reached up, beyond the ordinary, to touch the heart of her Lord.

A great cloud passed between the earth and the sun, then settled itself around the girl, embracing her in its softness, serenading her with its sweet harmony . . . and lifting her beyond the known into the mystery of its bosom. Pulsing with the beat of her heart, the sentient mist soothed the girl, filling her being with peace, with hope, with love beyond emotion. And then there came the voice . . . deep and sonorous, overflowing with lovingkindness.

"Greetings, you who are highly favored! The Lord is with you."

They were words, and they were not. More senses than sounds, rising like the swell of a great wave on the sea, caressing her heart before they reached her hearing.

"Do not be afraid, Mary." The voice took shape and stood before her, an angel more resplendent than a dream, more real than the earth, as glorious as the song of the morning. And she knew him at once as Gabriel, the messenger.

"You have found favor with God," he said softly, then paused, giving her time to touch and feel the idea of this statement.

The light that emanated from the angel intensified, suffusing the bright shadow in which they stood with a glow of gold and magenta, like the sky at sunset. Mary breathed in deeply, savoring the sweetness and power of the moment.

Finally, the angel went on. "You will be with Child and give birth to a Son and you are to give Him the name Jesus." Again, Gabriel paused until the enlightenment of Mary's heart became almost palpable. "He will be great and will be called the Son of the Most High," the angel continued. "The

Lord God will give Him the throne . . . He will reign forever . . . and His kingdom will never end."

"How will this be since I am a virgin?" Mary found her voice for the first time and wondered at its sound.

"The Holy Spirit will come upon you," intoned the angel, his words now seeming to Mary to be accompanied by a heavenly choir. "The power of the Most High will overshadow you, so the Holy One to be born will be called the Son of God." The mysterious choir soared toward a crescendo as the angel spoke his final words, "For nothing is impossible with God."

"I am the Lord's servant," Mary whispered to the receding light and the softening strains of the music which would live, from that day forward, forever in her heart. "May it be to me as you have said," her heart spoke to the departing angel.

After their ride, when Jesus had gone back to the carpenter shop to work on the box Joseph was helping Him make for Mary, Michael was drawn to the meadow.

"Mary?" Michael's voice was tentative as he approached her. "Are you all right?"

"Yes," Mary answered, "I'm fine . . . I was just . . . remembering."

"Are you sure? Was someone here with you? From across the meadow I thought I saw a great cloud, like steam rising from a hot spring . . ."

"A low cloud, perhaps," said Mary, looking away.

"Only that?" Michael sensed something more, felt some mystery lingering in the air.

"Come, join me for a while," Mary said, not answering his question.

"I don't want to disturb you."

"You could never do that. You're too kind . . . but you look troubled. What is it?"

"I'm not sure that I can explain." He paused. "It's just that sometimes I'm confused."

"You mean about Jesus." Mary's words were not a question.

"Yes, but how did you know?"

"He is a mystery," she said, again avoiding Michael's question. "At once so human, and so divine."

"How can this be?" Michael shook his head and shrugged his broad shoulders. "When I was a boy, younger than Jesus, my father began to teach me of the Son of God who would come to free the world from tyranny and hatred."

A wispy cloud floated across the sun and shaded the companions like a silken veil.

When Mary didn't respond, Michael went on, feeling he needed to validate his statement. "Because of what my father and the angel told me, I know that Jesus is this Savior. What I can't comprehend, is His humanness."

Still Mary said nothing. A shining blackbird with red and yellow epaulets on his wings perched on a rock near the spring and cocked his head to one side, as if preparing to ask a question.

"How can it be that this little Boy, who laughs and cries and loves just like any other must one day save the world?"

"Some things we are not given to know," said Mary at last. "Of all God's mysteries, Jesus is the greatest."

"But why must He live like any other?" Michael asked, not satisfied with Mary's answer.

"I think that it's important for Jesus to feel the hopes and the fears, the joys and the pains that are known by every man."

"But why?"

"I don't know, really." Mary hesitated. "Joseph believes that Jesus will be the advocate for every man and woman and child when He returns to His Father in heaven. For this, Joseph says, Jesus must know everything that we feel. Only by sharing our human feelings can He understand fully."

"And yet," Michael shook his head again, "there are times when it is obvious that He is divine. How can He be both mortal and immortal?"

"I think what you're seeing is what happens as Jesus learns about perfect and pure love."

"But what about the way He has with the animals?"

"Animals see things we don't. Without words, they talk to one another. I think they hear the voice of His heart, and understand."

"My mother told me that the animals are gifts from God," Michael said, his eyes bright with the memory. "She said God sent them to teach us about unconditional love . . . the kind of love that people don't usually share with each other . . . the kind of love that doesn't ask for anything in return."

"Your mother was very wise," said Mary, reaching over and touching Michael's hand.

"She told me, when I was really little, that God sent the horses to give us the wings of angels . . ." His voice trailed off.

Just then, there was a soft nudge in Michael's back. He turned to see Zabbai standing right behind him with Jesus on his back. "Where did you come from?" Michael rose from the ground laughing. "Were we so deep in conversation that we didn't hear You coming?"

Jesus jumped down and walked over to the pond where He splashed cool water on His face. "We sneaked up on you," He chuckled. "I told Zabbai to walk *very* quietly so that

you wouldn't know we were coming and we could surprise you."

"How do the horses . . . all the animals . . . know to listen to You when they don't listen to anyone else?" Michael asked, his mind still on the conversation he had been having with Mary.

"They know that I love them and wouldn't tell them to do anything wrong," Jesus answered. "All the animals are like the sheep that follow their shepherd . . . but won't go through the gate for a stranger."

"You make it all seem so simple," Michael said, shaking his head and smiling. "Let's go for another ride . . . put on those wings Your Father gave us." At that, he whistled for Esdraelon and the gelding came galloping through the tall grass toward him.

"You see," Jesus said, smiling, "you can talk to them too. It is a special gift My Father gives to a few He has chosen."

❧

Beside the Euphrates River, faraway, the horsemen moved their great sea of animals toward winter pasture. North of the main herd, a lone rider galloped after a pair of strays. A golden apparition, the horse and rider arose as one. From the arch of his elegant neck, the horse's flaxen mane streamed across the girl's face and mingled with her own fair hair, as those gossamer tresses were lifted by the wind to blend with the stallion's flying tail. Like the arc of an angel's wing, horse and rider glided across the uneven ground, leaping over treacherous chasms with grace that verged on poetry. In calm synchronization, the amber vision defied the earth, and triumphed.

Thrilling at the sight before him, John's heart ached for

his beloved sister, Junia, the only other horsewoman he had ever known who could rival this golden child. John had long been aware of the mystical alliance reserved by God for the girl, or the woman, and her horse. As he marveled at the melding of this particular horse and rider, John understood that in Adrianna, the daughter of Zimri the Healer, he was being given the opportunity to behold the archetype, the perfect example of this unique and lovely gift from God.

"Zimri . . ." John said aloud, shaking his head a little sadly, "if only you could see your beautiful daughter today."

The youngest of Zimri's sons and daughters, born long after the great horseman and his wife had stopped expecting children, Adrianna was the apple of her father's eye . . . and the one to whom he passed on his extraordinary gifts. For several years, until his passing the previous summer, Zimri spent every waking hour teaching his daughter the ways of the horse as he had not taught anyone since Michael. It wasn't that the healer had not wished to share his wisdom with his other children. It was simply that none of them had shown the interest or the aptitude that was Adrianna's.

Like Michael, the girl had poured her whole heart and soul into learning everything that Zimri could teach her, spending most of her time either working beside her father or quietly observing the herd. When she wasn't occupied in one of these ways, Adrianna studied training methods from Jephthah, the finest trainer of this tribe, the man who had taught Michael.

At eighteen years, Adrianna was well beyond marrying age, and her mother had long since given up hope that she would ever find such union. During his lifetime, Zimri had sternly scolded anyone who brought up the subject, assuring them that in her own time, his daughter would choose a husband and bear him fine children. Though he did not hold with the custom of the parents choosing mates for their children, in his heart of hearts, the healer could see no one with Adrianna except Michael, whom he had loved as a son. Only Michael, Zimri believed, was worthy of the radiant Adrianna. Though he did not often voice this sentiment, and never to his daughter, he created about the girl an aura of superiority that none of the young men of the tribe could breach.

For her part, Adrianna had heard such glorious tales of Michael, not only from her father but also from Jephthah, John and Sarah, that she was certain these elders had all become delusional in their dotage. After all, they were, in her mind, quite old. She thought that in Michael's absence, the elders must have built him up to be much more than he really was. She couldn't imagine that Michael could possibly possess all of the grand qualities ascribed to him. Besides, by now, he must be married.

Adrianna did recall the handsome, blue-eyed boy with whom her father spent so much time when she was a little girl. But her memories weren't especially kind. Her emotions in his presence had run the child's gamut. Sometimes she had looked at the older boy with childish love and longing. At other times she had felt only jealousy and resentment that her father cared so deeply for the boy and spent so much time with him . . . instead of with her.

Now, having collected the strays and reunited them with the herd, Adrianna rode to the top of a high mesa where she could look down on the field of horses and revel in the glory of sunset. Sitting astride Tamir, her palomino stallion, Adrianna wondered why, just now, thoughts of Michael invaded her mind. Then, as though an angel had answered her unvoiced question, she realized that since his passing, each time she brought her father to mind, Michael rode beside him. "Why can't he leave me alone with my father even now?" she asked aloud. "Why must he clutter up my memories of the man I will always love above all others?"

"Who are you talking to?" John asked as he rode up beside Adrianna.

"Tamir." Adrianna blushed. "I'm talking to Tamir, who always listens and never argues."

"It wouldn't surprise me if you taught this one to talk back," John said with a wry grin. "But have we failed you so badly?" His tone became more serious. "Can you not talk with us?"

"It's not that . . ." Adrianna paused. "It's just that I've never been good at talking to people . . . and with the horses, it's always been so easy."

"I knew a boy once who said that very thing," John whispered too softly for Adrianna to hear as he turned his horse and headed off toward the next hilltop. "I wonder," he added, "if the two of you will ever meet."

☞ MEANWHILE NEAR ANTIOCH ☜

"Junia," Archanus whispered to the darkening sky. "How I miss you, my sweet love."

"Was she very beautiful?" Rubria asked.

"Where did you come from?" Archanus tousled Rubria's long hair and smiled.

"I am never far away from you . . . I don't want you to be lonely."

CHAPTER
Twelve

CHAPTER Twelve

One afternoon, two years after their arrival in the mountain hideaway, Jesus and Michael were resting at their lookout point when a lone rider appeared on the delta below.

"Who can that be?" Michael thought out loud. "It's rare to see a man and a horse traveling this land alone."

As the horseman drew closer, joy began to light Michael's eyes. Though he could not see the rider's face, he recognized from a distance the carriage of the man, and of his horse. "It's John and Zadir," he said happily. "I've got to get to the foot of the hill and meet them."

"Don't you suppose the angels have brought him?" Jesus asked calmly.

"Perhaps you're right." Michael laughed at himself. "I've never known my mother's people to travel this far west, so he must have some special reason for coming here. I can't let him leave without a meeting!"

"I think he'll set up camp beside the river like My parents did when the angels first brought them here."

"Again, You're probably right. And I need to behave with as much sense as I did then. I'll stay here until I see that John has not been followed."

Michael's patience was sorely tested while the hours stretched out with interminable slowness. As uneasy as his nephew, John rode up and down beside the river searching for a crossing or signs of habitation. He had, indeed, been brought to this place by an angel who entered his dreams each night and gave him guidance for the next day's travel. But this day's ride had been short and neither the man nor the horse were exhausted enough to rest and await further instructions.

Finally, when dusk began to darken the delta, Jesus headed for home to tell Mary and Joseph the news. Michael climbed aboard Esdraelon and let the horse find his way through the brush, down the rocky hillside toward Lalaynia's switchback trail.

A year earlier, during one of their many explorations, Jesus and Michael had stumbled across this shortcut that enabled them to climb down from their lookout without returning all the way to their camp. Up until now, however, they hadn't had occasion to use it.

As Esdraelon carefully measured his steps along the rugged trail, Michael's thoughts drifted back to the long ago journey when he and his father escaped the Romans. He thought of the hillside where he and Archanus sat on the first night of their travels . . . at this same time of day, when the long shadows of evening at last lay down to await the dawn.

It was not that he hadn't observed this passage of day into evening a thousand times over the years. It was just that tonight he had a sensation of déjà vu~of having had an identical experience sometime before. So strong was the feeling that he kept turning to look behind him to see if his father was there. But he was alone . . . he was not really reliving that long ago day when he could look to his father for assurance and listen to his words wisdom. He could no longer hear the voice of his father and could scarcely remember that voice he had held in his heart for so long.

"What is it that I struggle to grasp?" Michael said aloud to the darkening sky. "Only the time of day and this trail are similar. What is this dread that grips me?"

Just then, Esdraelon's foot dislodged a stone and sent it tumbling down into the ravine. Again, Michael was carried back to a moment on the earlier journey when the tumbling of a loosened rock had been as fearful as an enemy attack. As though that terror stalked him again, Michael tensed and his heart began to race. Now, as then, through the curious, silent communication that passes between horse and horseman, Esdraelon felt his rider's panic and bolted in reaction.

Michael reached down and stroked the gelding's neck, laughing at himself and trying to calm the animal. "Like the face of my father," he said softly, "the fear is only a memory."

Reaching the foot of the steep, switchback trail, Esdraelon shook himself and drew Michael from his reverie. The azure sky glowed with the last vestigial warmth of the sun that had long since disappeared behind the western mountains. On the eastern horizon, the full moon of autumn was emerging. Giant bullfrogs croaked along the banks of the nearby river. Michael pulled Esdraelon to a halt, wishing to savor the scene, not ready to proceed.

The big bay stood calm, but alert, his head high, his nostrils flared, his ears foreward. Errant pieces of his black mane were lifted by the same gentle wind that rustled across the lush delta. Mesmerized by the swaying grasses, Michael recalled the words his father once quoted from an all but forgotten Hebrew text. "As for man, his days are like grass. The wind blows over it and it is gone. He withers like the flowers of the field, and his place remembers him no more."

"I remember you, my father," Michael whispered, his heart aching with the same fierce longing that lurked always just beneath the surface of his mind. "Please, dear God, give me peace from my yearning. I cannot carry this burden without You." Not since the epiphany in the meadow had Michael uttered such entreaty. In response, as if to remind him of that earlier release from sorrow and longing, the arms of the wind seemed to wrap themselves around him, enveloping him in peace and tranquillity.

The poignant sense of yesterday receded into memory, and for a time, understanding replaced confusion. Again, Michael recalled the words of his father. "Fine, strong minds," Archanus had warned, "sometimes struggle too valiantly, invent too much complication, when only in surrender can the riddle at hand be solved."

In the aftermath of his own struggle, Michael recognized his fear, all at once realizing that his uncle still symbolized parting and change. In this moment of clarity, he knew that as long as he lived he would not be able to completely forget that it was with John that his father had left him and that from that day forward his life had never been the same. It wasn't that John had been unkind or that Michael's life had not been good with the horsemen. It was only that John awakened in him a sorrow that he had struggled half a lifetime to put away. And yes, there was a chance of change in the very air that surrounded his uncle. If John came with word of Archanus, could Michael leave his present sweet life behind? Could he face another parting only to go in search of an uncertain future?

Again the breeze drifted across Michael's face and whispered its feathery calm. For just a moment, he dropped his chin to his chest in surrender. Then he looked up and moved on.

Arriving a few minutes later on the west side of the river, his handsome face illuminated by the huge and brilliant moon, Michael called across the water to his uncle. "John! Over here! Ride south with me and I will show you where you can cross!"

John could barely contain himself, so thrilled was he to recognize this boy grown into a man, the image of his father. For a quarter of a mile, John and Zadir galloped along the east bank following Michael and Esdraelon on the opposite shore, until finally Michael urged Esdraelon into the water and John followed his nephew's lead.

They met at midstream, clasped hands, then turned and lunged to the west bank. At the edge of the river, they jumped down from their horses. John wrapped his arms around Michael as though the handsome young man was still a child. "At last I've found you," John breathed, his words a salutation and a sigh of relief.

"I am so glad to see you!" Michael exclaimed. "It seems such a long time . . ." Stopping in mid sentence, he asked, "But why have you come? Is something wrong? Have you word of my father?"

"Nothing is wrong," John said, smiling and laying a calming hand on the shoulder of the statuesque Michael who had grown in height beyond his own.

"Everyone is well . . . and I have heard that your father is alive. But there's so much to tell you. Is your camp nearby?"

"We still have a long climb ahead of us, and the trail is sometimes both steep and treacherous."

"That must be why we were brought early to this impasse," said John, "so that Zadir and I could rest. We may come to regret our impatience."

"I hope not! I don't know if I can wait until we reach our destination to hear what has brought you."

"I'll tell you briefly before we begin the hard climb," John said. "I'll save the longer version of the story, though, until we reach your home."

"Thank you," Michael said, relief and gratitude plain in his voice.

John rode up beside Michael and began his tale.

"More than two fortnights ago, as we camped in the mountains near the northern arc of the Crescent, a shepherd boy wandered in for conversation. As always, Sarah asked if you had been seen by any of his people. He told us a frightening tale of one of his cousins who, some two years ago, was tortured by a vile Roman centurion into revealing the whereabouts of a small encampment where a single family and three fine horses lived and worked.

"We knew that he spoke of you because of his description of Lalaynia and Esdraelon. He told us also of a magnificent young stallion and though we were confused by this, we knew that precious few peasants share their homes with horses. We assumed you had acquired another in some way you would explain if only we could find you. We were terrified that harm had befallen you because we knew of Herod's continued treachery. Sarah would not rest until I came in search of you . . . and she will still find no peace until I return with word of your safety.

"When I arrived at what I believe must have been your old home place, I thought my heart would surely break."

Drawn back to that awful night, John went silent, seeing too clearly, the scene that had caused him such distress. . . .

❧

A small and obviously abandoned house huddled, lonesome and abject, amidst a field of grass grown taller than its low windows. No curtain hid from view the dusky, barren interior. A solitary owl called mournfully from somewhere nearby. Behind the house, a few hardy vegetables peeked out from between the weeds that ruled an abandoned garden. A noble tree stood alone on a bluff nearby, and a stream meandered disconsolately through the yard.

There were no signs of struggle, no evidence of destruction to the little encampment, just the horrible melancholy of a place left behind. No love lingered in the air, no peace, no hope. A sob, born deep in his chest, escaped John's lips as he fell to his knees, calling out to the One God and begging Him for some sign. "Let me know that they were here and that they are now safe," John entreated the night. "I cannot return to my wife with no more than I now know."

❦

"Are you all right?" Michael asked, alarmed by John's protracted silence.

Gladly returning to the present, John spoke at last. "Yes, I'm fine," he said. "Sometimes it's hard to escape our memories.

"That night, I fell into a fitful sleep, tossing and turning in an agony of sorrow . . . until the angel came. He told me of your escape and bid me to follow. Each night since then he has come with directions for one day's ride only. He never told me of my final destination, only directed me toward you."

"I am grateful," Michael said. "Very grateful . . ."

Just then, the trail narrowed and the riders had to begin their ascent. They climbed in silence, leaning forward to help balance and ease their horses' burdens. When they reached the summit, all was still. The full moon hung high, lighting the meadow as though it were day. Somewhere a night bird sang and crickets chirped their gentle symphony in the forest that rimmed the verdant meadow.

"Would you like me to continue with my news of your father?" John asked riding up beside Michael for the first time since they began their climb.

"I would like nothing better," Michael answered. "But you must be exhausted from your long journey. It's enough to know that my father is safe. I can wait until the morning to hear the rest when we can share the story with my friends." Michael's words belied his thoughts. He could barely wait to hear John's news. But he was too kind, too considerate, to disregard his uncle's obvious exhaustion.

Before tending to their own needs, the horsemen rubbed down their horses, massaged the animals' tired legs, and turned them out into the field where they could drink and graze. Only when these ministrations were completed did they retire to the cots Mary had made ready for them in the room Michael shared with Jesus.

"Your father is alive . . ." John's words sang a sweet lullaby to Michael as his own weariness carried him into fitful sleep. Drifting in and out of too real dreams, Michael met himself in the face of his father. Across the miles from yesterday to tomorrow, he galloped again beside the man who had given him life, hearing in the distance what he could only hope was the voice of God promising the reunion for which his heart could not cease to ache.

"So much is changing," said Luke wistfully. "It is as though our lives have gone out of control and we are rushing toward some madness that we cannot name."

Archanus and his students had chosen to spend the afternoon outdoors. They meant to concentrate on the lessons at hand, but they had not found it easy. Rubria's father, the Tribune Diodorus Cyrenius, had announced the previous evening that he was taking his family back to their old home place near Rome. Luke would soon be leaving to study medicine at the university in Alexandria. Archanus had been invited to go with Diodorus, but had declined, hoping that perhaps it was finally time to go in search of his son.

"My father will miss you even more than I will," said Rubria. "He depends so much on your wisdom . . ."

"And your mother depends on Archanus to keep your father calm." Luke laughed as he thought about the friendship between the volatile Tribune and the gentle spirited Archanus.

"We will all meet again," Archanus said, meaning it.

"Why not change your mind and accompany me to Alexandria?" Luke asked. "You have said you would like to see Egypt."

"Perhaps I'll join you there one day," said Archanus noncommittally.

"Perhaps . . ." said Luke.

CHAPTER *Thirteen*

CHAPTER *Thirteen*

They awoke the next morning to the smell of Mary's cooking and the sound of voices not far from their door. John arose first and stepped outside where he met Joseph.

"It's good to see you under less fearful circumstances than those of our last meeting," Joseph said in greeting.

"Good morning," Mary said. "We are very glad to have you join us."

"Thank you," John smiled at the beautiful young woman. Then some movement not far behind her caught John's eye. In the shadow of the house a Child, who looked to John to be in about His eighth year, stood near the most elegant young stallion the horseman had ever seen. "The shepherd greatly understated!" John chuckled, excusing himself from Mary and walking toward the beautiful Boy and His horse.

"He is Lalaynia's," Michael said, as he came up behind John.

"That is apparent." John continued to beam with profound and genuine pleasure. "But he far surpasses any foal she, or for that matter any member of our herd, has ever borne."

"He must be a son of Zadir," Michael offered.

"Yes, of that there is no doubt," John said. "His name?"

"Zabbai," Michael said.

"Ah . . . a gift from God," John responded, recalling the translation of the Hebrew word.

"Yes . . . Must he go back to the herd with you?"

"I didn't come to take this horse away," John said. "That is not the nature of my mission. I wonder though, he must have come into this world nearly eight summers ago. And yet he looks so young . . ."

"He was born exactly eight summers ago~not long after we settled in Egypt," Michael said. "I've often thought he was maturing slowly. But isn't this a trait of the gray ones?"

"Yes, it is," said John. "But he looks like a colt of three years or less. No other horse in my memory has ever matured so slowly."

"Zimri taught me that the greatest stallions always take the longest to mature," Michael said.

"And no one has ever understood these great creatures any better than Zimri," the horseman agreed before his full attention was captured by Jesus and Zabbai. Had John been asked to explain the reverent sensation he felt, he could not have done so. He only knew that a strange combination of absolute peace and limitless power emanated from the Child and that this aspect defied all mortal understanding.

Finally, Jesus broke the silence. "After we eat, will you come and watch Zabbai run?" the Boy invited. "Michael and I will race for you . . . so that you can see what a fine horse has come from your herd."

"I would love that!"

"It's not much of a contest." Michael grinned. "Zabbai is so fast and athletic that there's no way Esdraelon can compete with him . . . but they like to run together."

While the adults chatted companionably over the meal, Jesus fidgeted and played with his food.

"I don't know when I've seen You so excited," said Mary to her Son. "Run along to Zabbai, we'll be right behind You."

"A horse not so game as Esdraelon would have stopped rising to the challenge long ago," Michael shook his head and laughed as he swung up onto the big gelding . . . and then the race was on. Across the wide meadow they dashed, then circled back and with Zabbai far in the lead returned to the house where the onlookers clapped with pleasure.

"Show John some of the things You've taught Zabbai," Joseph suggested.

"Zabbai can do many things because My Father made him the smartest and most willing of horses," said Jesus, appearing embarrassed. "And Michael has shown me your ways of teaching." For the next several minutes, Jesus and Zabbai put on a dazzling performance with the stallion doing every kind of maneuver in response to commands that were virtually invisible in their subtlety.

"I've never seen anything like it!" John said, astonished and delighted after the race and the performance. "This horse is unbelievable . . . and with Jesus, the animal is like magic! I don't think I'll ever be able to describe this adequately. And even if I could, no one would believe me."

Afterward, Jesus and John rode out together, exploring and "visiting," as Jesus called it, with the woodland creatures. When they returned, John joined Michael and Joseph in the carpenter shop.

※

"This has been a wonderful morning," John said. "Zabbai is indeed the finest horse I have had ever the privilege of knowing. And Jesus is a horseman's inspiration! "

"Zabbai is a treasure. And, there *is* wonder in the Boy's touch," Joseph said, his voice filled with love and pride. "Now, please tell us of Archanus. Don't keep Michael in suspense any longer!"

"Almost a year ago, our old friend Zadoc came with his men to acquire mounts. We had not seen him for three seasons, and we feared the worst."

"How did Zadoc find you after all that time?" Mary asked.

"The soldiers know well our customary routes of travel," John answered. "They meet with us at about the same time every year to procure new mounts. Since we're creatures of habit, they don't have any trouble finding us."

"Where had Zadoc been?" Michael asked. "Why had he not come to you for such a long time?"

"I'm coming to that." John said. "As you may have heard, King Herod has gone gradually mad. Over the past few years he has had three of his sons murdered, and he remains all consumed with finding, and killing, the Child who was born beneath the Star."

Michael's heart skipped a beat as fear flooded over him.

"Zadoc," John continued, " traveled across the Great Sea to Rome where he sought audience with Caesar. It was his hope that the Emperor would depose Herod and replace him with a man of honor and sanity."

"Why did Zadoc assume this task?" Michael asked.

"Because of what he learned long ago from your father. Archanus, you will recall, told Zadoc of the coming Savior, just as he taught you of this Miracle. So, our good friend knew that the Child sought by Herod was the One for whom the world had been waiting. He wanted to do his part to protect this Child so that He might fulfill His purpose."

"Was Zadoc successful?" Joseph asked.

"Not in his efforts to have Herod deposed." John paused.

"Did he find my father then?" Michael asked.

"When Zadoc arrived in Rome, he learned that his old commander, Augustus Caesar, has declined in both health and wisdom. It seems that though he was a fine soldier, he is not so great a leader. Roman finances are in a state of disarray, and it soon became obvious to Zadoc that as long as the cruel Herod continues to support Roman taxation, he will retain his position in Judea. So, our friend failed in his efforts to have Herod deposed. However, something good did come of his journey. Returning from Rome, Zadoc traveled by ship to the island of Crete where he was given news of Archanus."

"Was Balthazar correct then?" Michael couldn't contain his excitement any longer. "Before the coming of the Star, the Magi heard that my father was keeping company with a respected Greek physician named Luke. Was this true?"

"Yes, in part," John answered. "Luke, it turns out, is a student whose teacher, Keptah the Chaldean, is a healer and member of your father's brotherhood. On the convoluted grapevine of information the story became twisted . . . perhaps purposefully to keep Archanus safe."

"Was my father in the country across the Great Sea?"

"Only for a short while. As it happens, Archanus has resided for some time near Antioch. And the real irony is that he has long been the guest of one of Zadoc's dearest old friends, the Tribune Diodorus, who is in charge of Syria."

"How has this come to be?" Joseph interjected.

"When Archanus left our camp many years ago, he traveled one of our customary routes through the Fertile Crescent that follows the Euphrates toward the Great Sea," John explained. "On his way to Greece, he stopped for a short time at Antioch. Keptah helped make arrangements

for his safe passage to that country beyond the Sea, where the wicked Herod held no sway. Archanus remained in Greece studying for three years."

"Why did he return to Antioch?" Michael asked.

"Because he knew it was almost time for the coming of the Savior," John said, glancing over at Jesus.

"But he did not come to the Birth," Michael said, still questioning, confused by this latest information.

"He was on his way toward the Star when he was accosted and wounded by robbers."

"How badly was he hurt?" Michael asked anxiously.

"The situation was grave," John said. "Had it not been for Keptah, he would almost certainly have died."

"Please, tell us the whole story," said Joseph.

"Keptah had tried to discourage Archanus from making the trip alone, but there was more even than the Miracle that drew him. He had told Michael to look for him beneath the Star. Archanus considered this a promise . . . one he was not willing to break.

"The night following Archanus' departure, Keptah had a vision in which he saw his friend being attacked. He convinced three soldiers to accompany him in following the route Archanus said he would be taking. When they found your father," John said, looking now at Michael, "he was near death. Had Keptah been a little slower in his response to the vision, or a little less skilled as a healer, I would not be giving you such good news."

"Is he really all right?" Michael asked, still fearful.

"Yes, he has recovered, though that recovery took a very long time."

"I still don't understand how my father came to be a guest of the Tribune Diodorus," Michael said.

"How *did* that happen?" Joseph wondered.

"Keptah is the healer who attends to Diodorus and his household. When your father became well enough to teach, though he still could not travel, he sought employment. Keptah told the Tribune of Archanus' great wisdom, and soon he was teaching the children of the Tribune's household. I am told that your father has since become the trusted confidante of Diodorus and the dearly beloved teacher of the man's children."

"And the one called Luke . . . is he a son of this Tribune?"

"No . . . but I have heard that he is loved as a son."

"But is Luke a healer?" Jesus wanted to know.

"No, he is a student who studies with both Keptah and Archanus," John answered. "According to Zadoc, he is extremely gifted and is devoted to Archanus."

"Has Zadoc seen my father?"

"Not yet." John paused. "He has learned all that he knows through a trusted soldier who serves under Diodorus. But he hopes to go back to Antioch to spend time with Archanus soon."

"Perhaps you wish to go with John when he leaves us?" Joseph said, a question in his tone. "You could then find Zadok and travel with him to the home of your father."

Michael did not answer, but left the carpenter and walked out into the meadow. His logical mind examining the problem from every angle, he kept walking and thinking . . . until at last he thought to pray.

His answer came in the words of the angel, *"You must find Mary and Joseph and provide them with safe passage into Egypt where you will remain as their protector until it is safe for them to return to their homeland."* The message was clear. No matter how his heart yearned for the long awaited reunion, he could not turn away from the responsibility he had been given.

He had been praying with his eyes downcast. When he looked up, Jesus stood before him. The brothers' eyes met, and Michael accepted once more the peace that surpasses understanding.

Together, they returned to the house. "I will not leave you," he said to Joseph and Mary. "I have been called to be your protector until that day when I can return you safely to your homeland. Only then will I go again in search of my father."

"You are, indeed, My brother," Jesus said, looking up at Michael and touching his hand. "You serve My Father well, and He will reward you."

❦

The next day, John made ready to depart. "Can't you stay for a few days?" Michael asked. "I long to hear of the horsemen and the herd . . . and you've only seen a small part of the meadow. The forest that surrounds us is most magical."

"I must return to Sarah. By now, she'll be beside herself with worry. I too wish that we had more time. But I'll be back with the herd soon. After we settle on the delta, I'll come here and we'll return together so that you can visit with our family, with no one the wiser about this hideaway."

"I'll await that visit with much hope, and not so much patience." Michael smiled at his uncle.

Jesus and Michael rode with John to the place where the switchback trail began its descent. "I'll be fine traveling alone," John assured them. "There is no need for you to come down the mountain only to return once you've reached the floor of the canyon."

"We will meet again," said Jesus. "Until then, go with God."

"Only my son was as fine a scholar as are you, Luke."

"That is the highest compliment I could receive." The student beamed at his teacher, then began to laugh with unbridled joy.

"What is this merriment?" The huge body of the Tribune filled the doorway, the joy in his eyes belying the gruffness of his words and his deep voice.

"I was just complimenting Luke on his scholarship," said Archanus, walking across the room to greet his friend.

"I have come to ply you with wine and promises," Diodorus said.

"What is it that you wish?" Archanus asked.

"I want you to remain in my household. I cannot imagine how we existed without you, and I do not wish to relearn this skill. I will pay you anything you ask!"

"Your offer is kind and generous. But I must go in search of my son," Archanus said. *"We have been apart too long. . . ."*

"Of course I would not dissuade you from this," Diodorus said, his tone far softer than normal. *"I thought you were leaving with Luke to attend the University."*

"But sir . . . I explained Archanus' mission." Luke sounded confused.

"I'm sure you did, Luke." Diodorus shook his head. *"I have become so impatient in this vile land that I only listen to half of what is being said."*

"I promise you that no matter how long we are apart, our friendship will go on," said Archanus, *"and one day we will meet again."*

The big man cleared his throat and turned away. *"The wine still awaits us. Come, let us toast the success of your mission."*

CHAPTER
Fourteen

CHAPTER *Fourteen*

The longest days of summer were past, and though the nights had not yet begun to turn cold, there was a change in the light and the air. The horsemen knew it would soon be time to take the herd down out of the mountains.

For generations, this hardy people had traveled with the sun and the grasses along the Fertile Crescent. It was their custom to winter close to the confluence of the Tigris and Euphrates Rivers near the northern edge of the arid Arabian Desert. In early spring, with an uncanny sense of what route would be best in a given year, they followed one of those waterways to its nearest mountain range where it was cooler and the grasses were plentiful. At the end of most summers, the horsemen would move the herd down out of the mountains and head back toward their usual winter camp. But this year, their leader, John, was considering a less favored route of travel and destination.

"We don't often winter in Egypt because none of us likes the trip!" declared one of the elders who sat with John at the night fire. The man's voice echoed his own anger and that of most of the others who were trying to convince John that he was making the wrong choice.

"I understand this," said John patiently. "But you must believe me when I tell you that the lush grasses of the Nile Delta are just what we need. We've overgrazed our usual pastures. We need to let that land replenish itself. I'm only talking about one season . . ."

For the past two summers, the horses had grazed on the grassy steppes of the mountains that formed the northwestern arc of the Crescent after their journey north along the Euphrates. The preceding fall, John had put one of his sons in charge of the herd, then traveled alone in search of his sister's son.

"In the past hundred years, we have only gone to the delta twice," another elder spoke up. "The last time was only nine years ago. It is too soon to go there again!"

Just then, their argument was prodigiously interrupted by the arrival of the horsemen's old friend, the Tribune Zadoc.

"Thank God you are creatures of habit," laughed Zadoc, stepping down from his tall, black horse. "If we didn't know your routine, it would be difficult to locate you when we need new mounts."

"Another reason not to change our course," said the first elder, looking smug and sanctimonious.

"Is there a problem?" asked Zadoc.

"I want to take the herd into Egypt for the winter, but I am alone in this desire."

"I know your people have never cared much for that enigmatic land. So why is it now your choice?"

"He says we've overgrazed our usual pastures," said the elder, scowling, "but we do not agree."

"He is your leader," Zadoc admonished in the firm tones of a military man. "He does not need to give you reasons for his decisions." Then, turning to John, he said more quietly,

"Where is Sarah? I long to hear her voice and enjoy the gentleness of her spirit."

"I think we'll find her near the stream," John said, smiling at Zadoc's apparent understanding of the need to talk in private. "Her heart aches with longing for Michael and she cannot bear these endless arguments, so she takes herself to a peaceful place and waits for me to reason with our stubborn kinsmen."

"You can tell me the rest of this story in her company," said Zadoc turning away from the night fire and the chagrined elders.

John was quiet until they had walked far enough away that no one else could hear them, then he began to explain. "I have found Michael in that region and I feel that I must take Sarah to see him before another winter passes."

"Is she not well?" Zadoc asked.

"She is healthy enough, but she has traveled many years through this life . . ."

"As have you, my friend, and you are the picture of robust health."

"Yes, but I have not borne five children. And sometimes she seems so tired . . ."

On a great rock beside the stream, Sarah sat humming a melancholy song. Her long black hair was laced now with strands of shining silver, but her body was still as slender as that of a young girl. At the sound of her husband's voice she turned, her dark eyes flashing with joy and recognition.

"Zadoc! How good to see you!" On her feet at once, Sarah rose on tiptoe to place a mother's kiss on the cheek of this dear friend.

"And you, sweet Sarah . . . you are as beautiful as ever. Not a line on your face, and the silver in your hair is but a halo."

"Oh how you do carry on." Sarah's face was bright with pleasure. "You and your flattery are always as welcome as spring flowers in mountain meadows! But what brings you to us, dear friend?"

"I have good news from the land of Judea and more to tell you about Archanus. I have finally come face to face with the man!"

"Is he well?" John asked anxiously.

"Yes! He continues his studies while doing much good in the community. His only sorrow is that he remains separated from his son."

"Time is strange." John shook his head. "It's been two years since you first told us that Archanus was alive . . . and it seems like that was only yesterday. Yet a hundred years might have passed since Michael and Archanus bid one another goodbye a decade and a half ago."

"The Jewish elders say that our lives are but a blinking of God's eye~they say that a thousand years in His sight are like a day that has just gone by." The soldier paused, looking embarrassed. "I'm sorry, Sarah. I know you're anxious for me to get on with my tale . . ."

"I love both your wisdom and your stories." Sarah said. "But come, let us make ourselves comfortable so that you can tell us everything."

In a grassy clearing a little further upstream, the companions sat down, each leaning against a rock for comfort. Then Zadoc moved into the tale he had to tell. A born storyteller, he set the stage, describing the scene and the events that led up to his reunion with Archanus. As he spoke, he was transported, along with his listeners, back to the setting he described. "My men and I were called to a meeting at Herod's Palace," he began.

The afternoon air was heavy and still, as it was so much of the time in the city of Jerusalem. Zadoc longed for the pleasant breezes that drifted from the Great Sea into the port of Caesarea each afternoon. The seaboard town had become for him a place of refuge away from the pervasive anger of Syria and Judea, where it was necessary for him to spend too much of his time. Along the sea, the acrid odors of incense and spices, olive, cypress and pepper trees were cleaned and softened by the damp, salt air. Inland, those same odors mingled with the heat and the heavy dust, intensifying their pungency until a man felt he must suffocate.

The suspicious eyes of angry Jewish priests and peasants followed the soldiers and their grand horses as they made their way through the town toward Herod's hillside palace. An occasional brown skinned slave child darted across the road in the fleeting defiance of youth. Each time such a child crossed his path, Zadoc cursed the endless injustices of this world gone mad and silently entreated the One God, in whom he desperately wanted to believe, to release him from the bonds of his own choosing. But the insistent noise of his discontent drowned out any answer the Tribune might have received to his entreaty.

"Why do you think we have been summoned to the home of Herod?" asked Octavian, the captain who had recently taken command of Zadoc's cavalry unit.

"I cannot imagine," answered Zadoc sardonically. "Herod has no love for me, so unless he plans some exquisite torture, like more years of service in an even hotter and more wretched land than this, I can think of no reason for his summons."

At the palace gates, Zadoc and his troops were welcomed with a display of groveling adulation. Zadoc turned toward Octavian and shook his head in disgust. In the courtyard, a cadre of slaves rushed to take charge of the soldiers' horses as the men dismounted. Half way up the sweeping marble stairway that led to the palace entrance a rotund soldier waited, watching Zadoc ascend, an unreadable expression in his tiny, porcine eyes.

"Delaturus," Zadoc nodded slightly, "what is this all about?"

"I see you have gained neither patience nor social grace," sneered the fat man.

"Never have I been summoned thus for social reasons," rejoined Zadoc. "I hope that my audience with Herod will take place immediately. I am anxious to return to my home beside the sea."

"You will be here at least a fortnight." Zadoc's old enemy, Delaturus, now the captain of Herod's palace guard, smirked maliciously.

Allowing himself and his two immediate junior officers to be led into the great hall of the palace, Zadoc said no more, recognizing the futility of conversation with this spiteful subordinate and wishing to avoid further aggravation.

In spite of himself, Zadoc was again impressed (as he had been on previous visits) by the ostentatious, yet elegant surroundings. Built in the most marvelous Greek tradition, the palace of Herod was a gargantuan polished marble edifice, completely encircled by tall, cool porches. All along the exterior promenade, slaves were stationed, their only purpose in life the waving of huge fans to keep the air moving, if not much cooler for its motion. The tall marble columns that supported the porch roof glistened pink and amber in the afternoon sun. The interior walls were inlaid with gold in artful, Greek patterns, and the footsteps of the soldiers echoed off the twenty foot ceilings as they followed their. corpulent guide toward the quarters they would inhabit while they awaited Herod's command.

For five days, the men languished in this opulent environment. Where politicians and social climbers spent their days in idle occupation and slatternly devotion to their vile leader, the soldiers yearned for purpose and action. While his men argued among themselves or sought distraction in the stables and the slave quarters, Zadoc's temper grew more and more intense. Finally, he could bear this lassitude no longer. Storming into the office of an unfortunate subordinate, the Tribune demanded audience with Herod.

"How apropos your timing," whined the effeminate young scribe. "The great Herod asked only moments ago that you be invited to join him. Come, I will show you into his chambers."

Zadoc followed the much smaller man's mincing steps toward the interior of the palace. In the first grand hall through which they passed, slave girls bathed and frolicked in glistening pools on either side of the long promenade. Beyond this was another immense room in which fat, bejeweled men reclining on luxurious pillows were waited on hand and foot by yet another army of sparsely clad slaves.

By the time he reached Herod's antechamber, the bile had risen in Zadoc's throat and he thought he would retch at the rank obscenity of this lifestyle he could neither justify nor abide. At last, before him a pair of massive, golden doors opened, and Zadoc could see across the vast hall a youngish man dressed in the finest purple velvet, perched high on Herod's throne.

"What is this ruse?" Zadoc demanded under his breath.

"Herod Antipas," the small guide shouted importantly, "I present to you the Tribune, Zadoc."

"Come forward," said the man in purple. "Approach me that I might speak with you in comfort."

Zadoc advanced. At the throne, he bent one knee and bowed in the soldier's stiff fashion. "I fear you have the best of me," he said simply.

"My father, King Herod the Great, has died," the young man said, then awaited response. But Zadoc did not speak and the silence drew out.

"Do you not have questions?" inquired Antipas.

"Certainly. I only awaited your command."

"What do you wish to know?"

"It would appear that you are the new ruler, taking your father's place."

"This is only true in part. My brother, Archelaus, is en route from Greece. He will sit on this particular throne, governing Jerusalem and the lands to the south in Judea. I prefer the cooler northern climates, and the sea."

"As do I, my liege."

"This is why I have summoned you."

Again, Zadoc waited.

"I wish you to take the position vacated by Diodorus. You will be the Tribune over Antioch. You may retain your home at Caesarea, but you will be required to reside closer to my own dwelling outside of Antioch. You will be Tribune over the area of Galilee and the Decapolis, all of which are under my command. Does this suit you?"

"Indeed," Zadoc inclined his head in deference and agreement. "When does this commission begin?"

"It has begun. You will go ahead of me to survey the territory. When my brother arrives, you will return to escort me to my new home."

"This is a very prestigious position," said John when Zadoc finished his story. "Are you not honored?"

"Yes, of course," Zadoc said with a sarcastic grin. "And I am grateful to serve Antipas, who is without doubt, the best of Herod's sons. He is so much different than his father and brothers, in fact, that I doubt his parentage. It is my guess that his mother found solace with some soldier and produced this particular son."

"I hope you haven't shared that opinion with anyone else," Sarah said, shuddering visibly.

With a look of concern, John took off his cloak and wrapped it around his wife.

"I'm all right," Sarah said. It's just the coming of night that chills me."

It was that time of day, after the shadows, when the soft light lingers, though its source is hidden from view. By that subtle illumination John could see the old grief that lay beneath the concern Sarah tried to mask. Too many losses of friends and family over the years had taken a toll.

"I have made this comment only to you, my dear friends, and to Archanus," said Zadoc, his eyes on Sarah. "Please, don't fear for me. I know well the ways of my world and I will protect myself."

"So, what of Archanus?" asked John, glad to draw Sarah's attention to a new subject. "You promised news of him. Did you actually see him on this journey?"

"I did!" Zadoc said. "He is well. And though he has suffered much, he has scarcely aged a day. But that's a long story, to be shared around the night fire after our stomachs have been warmed by Sarah's fine cooking."

The morning air was cool and fresh. War horses at rest grazed in an open field. Roman cavalrymen prepared for the beginning of a campaign. Beneath a tree, a man bent to the task of fitting iron shoes on the feet of the cavalry horses.

On a rock beside the stream that wandered through the pasture, Archanus breathed the heady musk of the animals and thought of his wife and son. Lately, he had been drawn each morning to this place where the calm of the great animals Junia had loved so well brought her back to him, even if only in memory.

"Archanus?"

"Come, sit with me, Luke. I am enjoying the horses and the sounds of morning," Archanus said, sharing only half the truth.

"I don't wish to interrupt, but I need your good counsel."

"You are never an interruption." A smile came to Archanus as he thought of the joy young Luke had brought him. "What is it that troubles you?"

"As you know, I am to leave for Alexandria soon. I am anxious to further my education."

"But?"

"But I feel it is not right for me to go just now, when Keptah is so heavily burdened."

"You speak of the illness that ravages the slaves and the poor of the city?"

"Yes . . . Keptah told me last night that it is the worst he has ever seen, or heard of."

Archanus fell silent as he recalled the awful plague that had taken his wife so long ago. "It was just such a misunderstood illness that changed my life forever," he said finally, unable to mask the anguish in his voice.

"I am sorry to remind you of your terrible loss."

The silence drew out until at last, Archanus responded. "Junia and Michael remain the lights in the dark night of my soul. Even sad memories are better than none at all."

"Knowing what can happen, you must agree that I should stay?" Luke said, still concerned with his dilemma.

"On the contrary . . . this pestilence is the very reason for you to go!"

"I don't understand."

"The more you learn, the more help you can be to future victims . . . and you must not expose yourself to the sickness that could take you, even as it did my wife."

"We are not sure of its contagion though."

"I am sure," said Archanus, his eyes downcast. "Keptah, too, is aware. Only the ignorant and superstitious refuse to believe what is right before their eyes."

"Who will help Keptah in my absence?"

"I will . . ."

"But you have been preparing to go in search of your son."

"This will have to wait. I feel the call of the One God, whom I have always obeyed. I will not abandon the good Keptah in this time of need . . . and I will not be part of the reason that you feel you must forsake your studies."

"I do not feel right about this," Luke said.

"Know that you too have been called by the One God. If you obey, you will one day know His reward."

Just then, Keptah arrived. "I have news!" he said. "The name of the new Tribune has been announced."

"And?" Archanus posed the question Keptah sought.

"It is your old friend!" Keptah paused. "The new Tribune is Zadoc!"

"When will he arrive?" Archanus asked, excited now.

"It is said that he will come within a fortnight.

"All the more reason for me to stay."

CHAPTER
Fifteen

CHAPTER
Fifteen

That evening, Zadoc told of his meeting with Archanus. Reminiscing in great detail, the storyteller carried his friends along, into the magic and the emotion of that visit.

❖

Harsh rays of sunlight glinted off swords and breastplates. The chink, chink of metal glancing off metal competed with the rhythmic pounding of more than a thousand hooves striking the ground. Dust rose in billows all along the line of mounted soldiers who rode four abreast before and behind the luxurious coach that carried Herod Antipas into the city of Antioch.

At the heart of the city, an oasis-like area spread out in all directions, pushing the buildings away from one another and offering a sort of plaza where people could meet in a clean and peaceful setting. In the park, a beautiful fountain brightened and cooled the air, its waters gushing joyously from their source, then cascading back down into the marble pool in a broad and glistening circle of dancing droplets.

Marble paths crisscrossed manicured grasses from the edge of the park to the fountain. Palm and olive trees shaded benches where men sat in conversation or repose. On the lawns, children played tag under the watchful eyes of their gossiping mothers.

At the edge of the park stood a tall, handsome man watching the army approach. At the head of the entourage, rode a man of great stature and power. As though beckoned by an irresistible force, the men's eyes met and locked even before they were near enough for actual recognition. Falling out of formation, Zadoc signaled Octavian to lead the march. Then, jumping down from his horse, delight warming his face and his eyes, he threw his arms around the man he had not seen for far too long. In a voice deep with emotion he asked, "My friend . . . can it be you?"

Returning the embrace, Archanus said softly, "It is I, dear Zadoc. It is I!"

Mysteriously, Zadoc's troops proceeded without so much as a glance toward their leader. When his carriage came abreast of the scene, even Antipas seemed not to notice that Zadoc had left his position. The moment was protected and somehow separated from all of the reality of the city and the entourage that announced its arrival with much noise and pomp and circumstance.

"I cannot believe my eyes!" Zadoc said. "I had heard that you were safe, but the news was hardly real until this moment!"

"Have you any word of my son?" Archanus asked, his eyes bright, his voice husky with a mixture of fear and hope.

"I have not seen him, but I have heard that Michael is well . . . a man grown . . . who serves the One God."

"Zadoc, do you realize that my son is now nearly the same age I was when he and I parted?"

"Can this be?" Zadoc said, shaking his head. "It seems like only yesterday that we escaped your pursuers. Where has the time gone?"

"It doesn't matter now," Archanus said. "Though my imagined crimes seem to have been forgotten, the One God has not seen fit to reunite me with Michael. Please, tell me everything you know about him . . ."

"I will," Zadoc promised. "Where can I find you this evening? I must return to my position, but as soon as Antipas has been installed in his new castle, I will escape that place and come to you."

"You too will have a new home," Archanus said, the hint of a smile softening his anxious countenance. "You will live in the fine house that belonged to the Tribune Diodorous Cyrenius when he held the post that is now yours. I have spent much time in that house and will meet you there."

For Archanus, the hours passed with agonizing slowness. Zadoc dispensed impatiently with the details he could not avoid until the captain who was his closest confidant carefully suggested that perhaps Zadoc need stay with his troops no longer.

"Thank you, Octavian," Zadoc said to the captain. "I know my mind has been elsewhere this afternoon."

"I can see that something important has your attention," said Octavian. "Should Antipas ask for you, I'll explain that you are about his business and tell him that you'll speak with him tomorrow. Do not worry. Sextus and I will handle everything."

"You are a good friend," said Zadoc, thinking he should more often show his gratitude to the young man who served him so well, and asked so few questions.

※

Having been directed by palace slaves to the estate that would now be his, Zadoc rode alone, trying to order his thoughts so that he could explain as quickly and completely as possible all that he knew about Michael. So engrossed was he that the tired soldier hardly noticed the graceful trees that rose in a high arch above the lane that led to his new home. Nor did he catch sight of the curious children peering out at him from behind those trees.

At the end of the long and beautifully landscaped driveway, a wide marble veranda surrounded a house fit for a king. Huge Doric columns in the best Grecian style supported a high roof. The setting sun warmed the white marble with hues of honey and mauve. On the steps at the front of the house sat Archanus, surrounded by a small army of children. At the sight of the lone rider, Archanus stood.

"This is your new master," he said to the children. "He is a good man, fair and honest and kind. You must serve him well."

Before any of the children could reply, Zadoc stepped down from his horse. Magically, an attendant appeared to take charge of the animal. Inclining his head toward the man, Zadoc said "Thank you," as the children scattered like the petals of a flower in the wind.

"Welcome to your new home," said a smiling Archanus.

"I would ask for a tour," Zadoc chuckled in response, "but I think we have more important matters to discuss. First, tell me what you have already learned."

"I know that my son attended the birth of the Savior," said Archanus. "I learned this from Balthazar. I know also that he parted company with the Magi soon thereafter. Beyond this, I know nothing. Please tell me, is he all right? Is he safe?"

"All right, yes." Zadoc paused and looked at his friend. "Safe? I cannot lie to you. Because he has chosen to serve the One God, he will never enjoy the kind of safety common to the less valiant."

"On the contrary." Archanus sighed, his eyes alight with joy. "Because Michael has chosen to obey the One God, he will always enjoy the true safety that can come only to those who make such choices."

"How I wish I could know this God as you do," Zadoc said. "Perhaps then I could finally find peace."

"It is yours for the asking, my friend. Be assured that the One God knows you. He is a generous God who does not use force but waits patiently for you to come to Him."

Archanus paused, giving Zadoc time to digest these truths before he pressed his friend for more information. "I am sorry to appear concerned only with myself when you are obviously in need of counsel, but I cannot check my burning desire to know more about Michael."

"You must not apologize. It is I who should ask forgiveness for not getting right to the story," Zadoc said, resting a hand on his friend's shoulder. "I will heed your words and one day soon find my way to the One God.

"Now, about your son . . . As I told you, I have not seen him, and what information I have is not really current."

"Any news is better than none at all," said Archanus anxiously.

"Some nine years ago, while you lay wounded and under the care of the healer, Keptah, your wife's people encountered Michael. The boy was traveling with a man and wife and their Baby Boy, headed south along the Great Sea from Gaza.

"I don't know the details of how this came to be," Zadoc went on, but according to John, after Michael parted company with Balthazar, he was visited by an angel who sent him to Jerusalem on a mission for the One God."

"And that mission was?"

"I'm not sure how much you know of what went on after the Star disappeared."

"When I recovered, Keptah and Luke brought me up to date, at least in regard to everything they knew. Do you refer to Herod's edict to murder all of the male children under the age of two years?"

"Yes . . ."

"So, my son helped a certain Family escape this awful fate . . ."

"Yes."

Archanus grinned broadly, the light of his joy filling his eyes. "My prayers have been answered," he said. "My son has been given to do what I could not. But tell me, Zadoc, is this the last you have heard of him?"

"It is the last certainty."

"But is there more?"

"Some years ago," Zadoc began, "Herod sent soldiers to Egypt in search of the Child born beneath the Star. A wicked centurion by the name of Carvillius tortured a shepherd and learned of a Family living somewhere on the Nile Delta with a horseman and three fine horses."

"What came of this? Were they found?"

"We cannot be certain, but Octavian, the man who is now captain of my cavalry, was among the soldiers assigned to Carvillius after that wretch's mistreatment of the shepherd. I would trust Octavian with my life and, though he did not see Michael, he feels certain that he did come in contact with the Child's parents."

"But what about Michael and the Child?"

"Octavian believes that they had escaped prior to the soldier's arrival at their home."

"What made him believe he encountered these people and not some other family?"

Zadoc paused before answering. Finally, he said, "Octavian is a man of faith. He knew of you and of the Prophecy. . . . Though there was no tangible proof, he has tried to explain to me a *knowing* . . . not unlike feelings you have attempted to share with me in the past."

Archanus fell silent, his mood abruptly changed. "I fear that if Michael is, in fact, still living with this Family, he is soon to have his heart broken yet again," he said at last, shaking his head sadly.

"I don't understand."

"In order to fulfill His destiny," said Archanus, "the Child born under the great Star must return to the land of Judea. As long as Herod remained alive, it was not safe for the Boy. Now, with Herod gone, the Child must go back to the home of His forefathers."

"How do you know this?"

"In the same way I knew of His birth," Archanus said simply.

"How will the Family know of this?"

"The parents are aware of the Boy's divinity and His mission. When they are given the information that Herod is dead, they will know what they must do."

"And I am to pass on this information?"

"You too will know what to do," said Archanus mysteriously.

"Why must Michael's heart be broken?"

"I think that he will not be able to remain in the company of this Family, so he must face another parting."

"And do you have reason to believe this, or are we back in the realm of mystery?"

"In this case, logic and mystery share the stage."

"I will go to the horsemen at once," said Zadoc. "I know what I must do . . . and they will know their part."

"So you have come to us to carry this message to my nephew?" said John, only the hint of a question in his tone.

"Yes," Zadoc answered.

"What makes you think we know how to find Michael?"

"We have all been connected~you and I, Archanus and his son~in a strange way for some great purpose. It was Archanus who first explained this to me long ago. Since then, I have come to believe that this One God of his is the same God worshiped by the Jews. I have even sought Him in their synagogues. And I believe that I have been both visited and protected by His angels."

"We too believe," offered Sarah looking pointedly at her husband. "And we trust you!"

"I know that it is a great responsibility," Zadoc said softly. "And I do not want to know anything more from you. I am merely a soldier telling old friends of political events. What these friends do with the information is none of my affair."

"What you ask of us is a great honor," said John. "But why do you not make the journey yourself?"

"I could not travel far from my post just now . . . even if I knew where to search. I do not trust Archelaus, and I must see to the well being of Antipas. Besides, it is still not safe for me to have information about the Child. Should any questions ever arise in His regard, it would be best that I, a Roman Tribune, not be able to place Him in danger."

"We understand," said John. "I will prevail in the argument to winter this year in Egypt. While there, I will make the necessary contacts."

"Isn't it interesting," mused Sarah, "how all of these journeys and meetings occur just at the right time to fit perfectly together. . . ."

For the next several days, the Roman horsemen tried out new mounts and the infantrymen who wished to join the cavalry competed in the customary games to prove their worthiness. While this went on, John and Zadoc had the opportunity to visit. Without revealing their exact location, the horseman told the soldier about Michael and his adopted Family . . . and the magical land where they lived.

The day after the Romans left, the horsemen began their long trek toward the Great Sea to the valley of the River Nile. On the morning following his first meeting with Zadoc, John simply laid down the law for his people.

"As your leader," he said, "I choose to winter in Egypt. We will begin our journey as soon as the soldiers have purchased their new mounts."

In the face of John's stern command, no one argued.

MEANWHILE NEAR ANTIOCH

In a dim and cool room, a man lay silent, his breathing strained, his heartbeat fast and weak.

"I fear for the life of our dear friend," Archanus said.

"But Keptah has always been so strong," Luke said, confused and disbelieving.

"He is no longer a young man . . ."

"He cannot succumb," Luke pleaded. "The disease has run its course. There have been no new cases in almost a fortnight. How can this happen?"

"If it is God's will for Keptah to leave us, we must let him go," Archanus said, laying his hand on Luke's shoulder.

"I will not let him go without a fight," Luke said resolutely. "I will do no less than he would do for me . . . or for you."

"He has taught you well. No matter the time of his departing, you will carry him with you always in your heart."

CHAPTER
Sixteen

CHAPTER
Sixteen

A breeze wafted across the hot land. The sun hung heavy just above the western horizon. Golden light glistened on the Great Sea as it surged toward the shore. Arms of the Nile River snaked toward that same shore where their waters would blend anonymously into the Sea. Tall grasses waved as the damp wind passed over the delta. And the only sign of autumn was a slight cooling of the humid air.

Into the silence, a low sound began to build and the small creatures that lived beside the rolling waters felt a deep rumbling in the ground. Soon the air was alive with the thundering of hooves as the horsemen urged their enormous herd toward its winter home.

Around the perimeter of the herd, twenty men and one young woman rode, keeping the horses together, not allowing any to stray. Some distance behind the main herd, three wagons rolled noisily along carrying the horsemen's goods and tents. Some of the tribe's women drove wagons, while others rode along beside. Five mares with foals born late in the season were also part of this entourage.

After Zadoc and his men left their summer camp, John had led his people and his horses on a slow and steady journey along the Great Sea toward winter pasture in the Nile River Delta. On this final afternoon of the long trek, he decided to let the horses stretch their legs and gallop into the big meadow where they would rest and graze before moving further west. Traveling just ahead of the drive, he chose a stopping place, turned his horse and signaled the other herdsmen to bring the animals to heel. With the deftest and most subtle of motions, the outriders began to circle, bringing the herd skillfully under control. Soon the horses slowed to a walk before dropping their heads to taste the sweet delta grass.

❧

That night, when all was quiet, John spoke to his wife of Adrianna and Michael. "It may at last be time for these children of destiny to meet. I wonder . . . do you think the girl has forgiven Michael for the favor her father once showed him?"

"I think so," Sarah said, pleasure in her tone. "I know she dreams of him because his name keeps sneaking into her conversations . . . especially on this journey. Did you tell her that we might see him in Egypt?"

"Yes," John answered, sounding guilty. "I thought I had to. She came to me, asking that I change my mind about our winter destination. Some of the herdsmen, it seems, convinced her she should intervene. I didn't know how else to explain. . . ."

"You did the right thing," Sarah assured him. "Adrianna has always been wise far beyond her years and one day, she'll be an elder of our tribe."

"Do you really think she's dreaming about Michael?"

"Why would she dream of any other?" Sarah teased. "We have all pushed her in that direction since she was old enough to toddle."

"We haven't . . ." John was chagrined.

"Oh yes we have, especially her father . . . and what would be wrong with that? There have never been two more beautiful youngsters, nor two who understood the horses as well as Adrianna and Michael do."

"That is so true," John said, then shared with his wife the awe he often felt as he watched Adrianna and her horse seeming to fly across the land. "Except for the amber color of her eyes, she is so like Junia . . ." John's voice trailed off and for a time he was quiet. "I wonder if Michael will see his mother in the girl as I do?" he said finally. "And if he does, I wonder if he will be drawn to the resemblance or frightened by it?"

"Soon we will know." Sarah assured her husband. "In God's time, everything works itself out. We cannot control the lives of our children as we do the movements of the herd. We can only pray for the best . . . and not be too disappointed if God's will doesn't always match our own."

At the lookout point on the eastern edge of their hideaway, Michael and Jesus sat in companionable silence, watching the delta below.

"Do you think the horsemen will come this year?" Jesus asked.

"Do You always know what I'm thinking?"

"Not always. Sometimes it's just a matter of that simple logic for which your father's people are famous."

Michael smiled with deep affection and shook his head. "I don't know if the horsemen will come. It is my hope. But most of them don't care much for Egypt. So even if John chooses the delta for winter pasture, he may have something of a fight on his hands."

"Do you long for your people?"

"You and Your parents have become my people." Michael looked into the eyes of the Boy who had come to mean more to him than any other human being, ever. "I do long to see my father . . . and it would bring me joy to ride again beside the herd. But the great need I once felt for reunion is not so painful now."

Warm light filtered through the trees and surrounded Jesus. At His feet beside Shadow, a chipmunk and a raccoon nibbled on the sweet berries He always brought to feed the forest creatures. Behind Him, a buck deer and his doe grazed with Zabbai and Esdraelon. The afternoon wind had begun to drift through the trees, its melody building toward one of those symphonies of nature that could often be heard beneath and between the words of Jesus.

In the luster of approaching dusk, tiny golden particles created a shimmering aura around the Boy. Strands of bronze and pale mahogany mingled with the tawny gold of His tousled hair.

Michael sat beside his adopted Brother, relishing the peace that suffused the air around Him. And again, as he did so often, the young horseman marveled at the gift he had been given. "Why have You blessed me thus?" His mind reached silently toward the One God.

"It is not the reason that matters," whispered Jesus in response to Michael's unspoken question. "Be thankful only that you were chosen as I am thankful that you obeyed."

Michael looked again into the ancient eyes, mirrors of forever that contradicted the age of the Child. "I must tell You that sometimes I doubt . . ."

"You doubt what you cannot see," Jesus said ruefully. "So many will not believe . . . even when they see and hear and feel the miracles . . ." His voice trailed off and He gazed for long moments at Zabbai and the world beyond the great stallion. "One day, a long, long time in the future, I will return, riding Zabbai and leading an army of avenging angels into the final battle."

"I do not understand," Michael said. "What will happen before then~to You and to Your mother and father? I have come to love you all so much. And I fear what may lie ahead . . . for all of us."

"I must do what My Father has sent Me here to do . . . and you must go back to the horses where your own mission will continue."

"What is it that You have been sent to do?"

"I have come to teach the world of love . . . to show that only this matters, and nothing more."

"Why can I not stay with You?"

"The work we have to do, we can only do separately."

"Why must this be so?" Michael asked, a lump forming in his throat as he recalled the too similar words of his father spoken so long ago.

"Because it is My Father's will."

"I am afraid," Michael said, "afraid of living this life without You."

"Do not fear," Jesus said tenderly, "You have found the Way and you will walk in it, as will your children and your children's children."

"I cannot imagine myself as a father. There is too much agony in loving, too much uncertainty. How can anyone face such danger to the heart?"

"The only real danger is in not loving," said Jesus, looking deeply into Michael's eyes.

"I know that Your words are true. I only wish that I could feel this truth as clearly as I hear it."

"You will know the truth, and the truth will set you free," Jesus said. "You will love and be loved, and you will beget more fine horsemen such as yourself~children with the intelligence of your father and the wisdom of your mother, children who will carry on both traditions. Where I must go, this would not be possible.

"One day I will need you in a way we cannot know just now," Jesus continued, resting His small hand on Michael's as though He were the adult and Michael the child. "When that day comes, My Father will again bring us together."

Michael pulled the Boy into his strong embrace, then bowed his head and clung to Jesus.

"I will be with you always," Jesus whispered.

The waning light throbbed with new force, coloring the meadow in brilliant rainbow hues. The symphony of the wind in the trees surged to crescendo. Jesus stepped back then and the brothers' eyes met. In that moment, all of Michael's past gave way to his future, and the horseman knew the power of the blessing he had just received.

❧

In the forest, birds sang as they flitted from tree to tree. The creatures of summer gathered food in preparation for the change of season. Somewhere off in the distance an owl awoke and called to its mate. Zabbai and Esdraelon grazed peacefully, emitting now and then a little snort of pleasure.

At the house in the meadow, Mary prepared the evening meal, tears slipping silently down her cheeks. Finished with his work, Joseph came to the house to ask if Mary needed anything from the garden.

"What is it?" he asked when he saw her tears.

"I do not know," Mary said, shaking her head. "I have a strange sense of foreboding . . . but I do not understand why."

"I too have been uneasy today," Joseph confided, putting an arm around his wife.

"Perhaps God is preparing us for some change." Mary said, moving closer to Joseph for comfort.

The sun had dropped behind the trees so that all of their small world rested now in shadow. Day birds caroled their farewell and the nocturnal animals began to stir. Chirping crickets joined the noisy frogs as the song of the evening began. Here in the mountain hideaway, the autumn air held a new chill. The sweet odors rising from Mary's cooking fire drew Jesus and Michael, warming them and bidding them welcome.

While they shared the evening meal, they talked of many things, as though each wished to forget some fear through steady conversation. Everyone, except Jesus, found it hard to sleep and the three adults all awoke before the dawn.

"I'm going to ride down to the delta today," Michael announced as the trio stood warming themselves beside the morning fire. "I think Jesus should stay here. I have an uneasy feeling . . ."

"I think you will find your kinsmen today," Joseph said.

"I have wondered about this as well." Michael relaxed a little. "I hope this is the reason for my anxiety, and not something more perilous to you and to Jesus." Then he swung up on Esdraelon's back and prepared to leave.

"Travel safely," Mary said, reaching up to touch Michael's hand. "We will pray for your reunion and anxiously await your return."

Jesus sat aboard Zabbai waiting patiently. He had not asked to accompany Michael but said He would like to ride

along to the switchback trail. They turned, and rode toward the sun. Exchanging no words, they moved in companionable silence.

"Go in peace," Jesus said, His eyes bright, when they reached the place where they must part. Michael nodded his head, then he disappeared over the ridge.

⌒ MEANWHILE NEAR ANTIOCH ⌒

"Since Keptah died, you have not been yourself, my teacher," said Luke. "Is this sadness too great?"

"It isn't that," began Archanus. "I believe that Keptah has gone to a better place. Of course I miss him. But more than this, his passing has made me wonder again why the One God has left me on this earth. Why have I not been taken at any of the times I have been in such danger?"

"You have taught me that always this God has a plan for us. Where is your faith in your own time of need?"

"A point well-taken," Archanus responded.

"Perhaps if you will pray as you so often suggest I do."

"Of course you are right . . . I will ask for His guidance."

"Archanus." Zadoc's deep voice called from the hall outside the classroom where Luke and his teacher sat talking.

"In here . . ."

"I have news! I have just come from my meeting with the horsemen and I have learned more about Michael!"

"Come and sit with us," Archanus invited. "Tell us everything!"

"Remember the shepherd I told you about, the one who fell into the hands of the evil Centurion Carvillius?"

"Yes . . ." Alarm was plain in Archanus' voice.

"One of the unfortunate shepherd's kinsmen carried the tale to your wife's people. It seems that the horses have become legend.

. . . *especially a young stallion. In any case, the story alarmed John and Sarah, and Sarah insisted that John go in search of Michael to warn him of the danger."*

"And . . ."

"John journeyed to Egypt and found the rumor to be true."

"What rumor?" Luke asked, his confusion obvious.

"It is said that a handsome young horseman is the protector of the Child born beneath the Star."

"Michael?" Luke asked.

"Yes, what I have heard from my friend, Octavian, and others leads me to believe that Michael has been living with the One Archanus has so long awaited."

"So they are in Egypt!" Luke said, jumping up from his chair and striding across the room. "Now, Archanus," he said turning, his face a mirror of excitement, "you must go with me to Alexandria! From there we will go in search of your son!"

"Wait, it's not that simple," Zadoc said. "Michael and his adopted Family have moved on. They now live in what John calls a 'mystical land found on no map, somewhere beyond the River Nile."

"Does John know how to find them?" Archanus asked.

"Yes, but by the time you arrive in Egypt, they may well be gone. Do not forget the message I took to John, which he in turn was to deliver to this Family."

"Nonetheless," said Luke firmly, "we must make this journey without delay!"

"Luke is right," said Archanus. "Will you come along?"

"There is nothing I would rather do. But I still cannot leave Antipas."

"I understand," said Archanus, recognizing Zadoc's reluctance, and his sense of duty. "We must prepare to leave. One day, my friend, we will meet again."

CHAPTER
Seventeen

CHAPTER
Seventeen

L ater that day, Michael arrived on the mesa overlooking the grassy plain where the herd and the horsemen were headquartered. His heart pounded heavily in his chest as he approached. "How will they receive me?" he wondered. "Will I be welcomed by them all, or only by my aunt and uncle?"

John was the first to recognize Michael as he rode toward the encampment. "Sarah, come quickly!"

All but running toward their nephew, John and Sarah led the way to where the young man was respectfully dismounting before entering the camp. Michael's fears were put to rest when all of the men and women gathered round him, everyone talking at once, their voices filled with love and welcome.

When the little crowd finally began to quiet a big man came forward and wrapped his arms around Michael. Recognizing his beloved teacher, Michael returned the embrace, laughing to conceal the tears of joy that welled up in his throat.

"Jephthah! You have not changed! Not aged one day! How is this so?"

"I am at peace and I am healthy. But you . . . you have changed for us both! You were a boy and now you are a man. I would take you for your father, before I would know you as his son!"

"If only I were so wise as he . . ."

"You have always underestimated your gifts."

"You're just in time for the afternoon meal," Sarah interrupted, then smiling up at Michael, she took his arm to walk with him toward the camp. "Come eat with us. You and Jephthah can continue your conversation, and you can tell us all about your life."

"Michael, how did you know that we would be here?" John rejoined the conversation. "I was planning to come looking for you once the herd got settled."

"I didn't know. I just felt the need to come here today."

"The mysteries that have always surrounded you never cease to amaze me." John shook his head in wonder.

Over the meal, Michael made polite conversation for as long as he could before asking for news of his father.

"We have heard that all remains well with Archanus," said John. "Before we left the northern mountains, we were visited by Zadoc who gave us much news. But we should talk of these things this evening, after all is quiet."

Though Michael was anxious, he would be patient, understanding that John was being careful with whatever information he had to impart. "I would like to walk through the herd," he said. "It has been so long . . ."

"Of course." John said.

"But what of Zimri?" Michael asked, all at once realizing he had not seen the healer. "Has he stayed among the horses as he so often does instead of eating with the others?"

"I'm sorry," said John, "we should have told you. Zimri passed on soon after I returned from my last visit with you. He was an old man . . . and he had lived a good life."

Michael took in a deep breath, then looked off across the herd, his heart filling with memories of Zimri, the healer who had taken him under his wing, treating him as his own son. Thoughts of Zimri's wisdom and his kindness competed with Michael's fear that his own father would succumb to age and illness before they could meet again.

"I'll go to the horses now," he said simply. No one spoke as he walked toward the herd.

Across the valley, a lone rider sat atop a hill observing the herd and the new arrival. "He is here," said the girl stroking the neck of her horse. "I wonder how he will feel when he hears that my father is gone? I wonder if we will know one another? I wonder if he is real, or only the illusion of those who love him?"

For hours, Michael walked among the animals, running his hands over a smooth back here, touching a beautiful face there, recognizing the older mares, and marveling at the strength and beauty of the young ones. In a little clearing where the grass was low and dense, he sat down as he had long ago learned to do and waited for the curious foals to approach him.

First came a small sorrel filly with the loveliest eyes he had seen since Lalaynia's. Walking with a kind of careful boldness, her neck low and her ears forward, the filly reached out and tickled the back of Michael's neck with her tiny muzzle. Dropping his chin lower to expose more of his neck, he grinned with pure joy at this sensation he had not felt for so long. Soon a big black colt, followed by a bay and a dun filly, and two more sorrels, were gathered around him, sniffing and sneezing and touching. His face and eyes were alight and he was chuckling softly when the girl approached.

"Don't get up," she said in a sweet, melodious, and somehow familiar voice. "They are enjoying you too much to disturb them."

Startled by the arrival and amazed that the foals did not share his alarm, Michael could only stare in confusion at the intruder. With the lowering sun behind her and her head bent, her facial features were difficult to discern. Her long, golden hair, backlit by the sun, spread out like the shimmering wings of an angel. For just a moment, Michael felt some deep pang of recognition.

"Where did you come from?" he stammered.

"For a while I watched you from the hill. Then I rode down to get a closer look. I've been watching you from within the herd since you sat down to play with the foals. I am Adrianna. And you, I presume, are the famous Michael."

"How do you know this?"

"You do not remember me . . . but I would know you anywhere."

"I'm sorry."

"Why? I was just a small girl when you went away. Why should a handsome boy like you have noticed me . . . especially when you were so involved with my father's teaching?"

"Were you Zimri's beautiful little daughter with the flashing eyes who hated me because I stole your father's time?"

"One and the same." She and her flashing eyes laughed.

Finally, Michael stood up and the foals began to drift away. Because he was so much taller than Adrianna, she had to tip her head back and look up to meet his gaze. In one of those rare and wonderful moments of complete recognition, their eyes locked. Their breathing synchronized in a mystical union, and time stopped while each became acquainted with the sense of the other. Like dancers in a dream, they moved in stillness, one heart straining toward the other, two minds joining to advance as one.

In time, the handsome young man and the beautiful girl turned to walk side by side into the herd. They spoke as though resuming a long suspended conversation in a way that two people who had known each other always might reminisce. At the edge of the herd, Adrianna's golden stallion stood grazing quietly beside Esdraelon as though they too had always been herd mates.

"They are brothers," said Adrianna, seeing Michael's slight puzzlement as he assessed the similarities between the two horses. "Esdraelon was the first of their mother's foals, Tamir the last."

In wordless agreement, the new friends swung up onto the backs of their horses and urged them into a gentle lope. Across the meadow they glided until they reached the river where the horses turned on their own toward the crossing. Adrianna's lithe body melded smoothly with that of her horse. With gentle hands and long, elegant legs, she guided Tamir with almost imperceptible commands. Like Michael, she asked the animal to do her bidding, never insistent, never demanding.

Beyond the water, they climbed into the hills exchanging a few words now and then, but remaining mostly quiet, reveling in their unspoken understanding. Where the trail became steep, they gave the horses their heads and allowed the surefooted animals to choose their own trail. No matter how powerful the upward surge, no matter how long the leap, neither the man nor the girl was

ever unseated. Instead, each horse and rider were as one in a connection that defied the earth and breached the sky. Finally, atop a wide mesa, the riders stopped to survey all that lay below.

"A strange land, this Egypt," Adrianna said.

"Not a favorite of our people," Michael added. "Was there great argument when John decided to come here this winter?"

"There was . . . until John would broach no more discussion. Even though he told me we would meet you here, I wondered why he was so insistent. Now I know."

"And the answer?"

"So that we could meet . . ."

"Once again, John made the right decision."

When they rode into the camp that evening, Michael and Adrianna were greeted by knowing looks and smiles. No one teased or questioned. Instead, everyone looked smug and satisfied as if some prophecy had at long last been fulfilled.

For two more days, Michael remained with the herd, riding out with Adrianna, sharing her chores, coming to understand that her skills as a healer were even greater than her father's had been.

"She is not only the finest healer any of us has ever known," commented Jephthah as he and Michael observed Adrianna's ministrations on the second afternoon, "she is also a rider and trainer of such extraordinary talent that she is unequaled by anyone other than you."

"Neither of us will ever be your rival," Michael responded modestly.

"Not so!" Jephthah said placing an affectionate hand on Michael's shoulder. "In this case, the students by far exceed the teacher . . . and I am very proud."

That night, over the evening meal, Michael announced that he must leave. So engrossed had he been in Adrianna, that he had never asked John to finish telling him of Zadoc's visit.

"I would like to ride with you," John said when he and Sarah and Adrianna had been left alone at last with Michael. "And I think Adrianna should come along."

"A grand idea," said Michael, smiling. "But what of Sarah?"

"I'll be fine right here," Sarah assured him. "I need to stay where it is warm, and riding is no longer so easy for me. I would only slow you down. Besides, I know that John and Adrianna must return to the herd soon."

Placing a loving arm around his wife, John said, "Michael will be back one day too . . ."

❧

The next morning, the three companions left before dawn. They covered ground quickly at the long trot, riding in silence for many miles before stopping to rest the horses and share the light snack that Sarah had packed for their journey.

John had insisted on presenting Mary and Joseph with horses of their own, so both Michael and Adrianna led an additional animal. For Mary, John had chosen a beautiful little chestnut mare named Larissa, a granddaughter of Lalaynia. For Joseph, he picked out a stout black gelding called Jericho. So like Ghadar was this young gelding that Michael couldn't help remembering the dear old war horse that had traveled with him and Lalaynia on their journey to the birth of Jesus.

"You seem more careful than ever with information," Michael said to John as they rested beside the river. "Is there someone among our people who cannot be trusted?"

"Our kinsmen are as trustworthy and honorable as ever." John paused. "It's just that I don't want anyone to be endangered because they have too much knowledge."

"Like the shepherd," Adrianna offered.

"Yes," said John. "I wonder, now, if I have made the right choice bringing you along."

"Don't worry." Adrianna assured them. "There is no horse in the land that can best Tamir in a race. He will take me to safety if ever the need should arise."

After their short break, as they rode toward the canyon and the switchback trail, John at last began to tell Michael of Zadoc's visit. By the time they reached the rugged path, Michael had begun to understand what lay ahead for him and for his adopted Family and was amazed again at the way Jesus sometimes seemed able to see into the future.

Just beyond the ridge, where the steep trail met the meadow and the thick conifers gave way to open expanse, Jesus and Zabbai greeted the three tired riders and their incredibly still fresh horses.

"How did you know we would come today?" Michael asked, his eyes alight with joy.

"I didn't know for certain," Jesus replied. "I only hoped." Shadow sat alert, but quiet, on a large boulder near Jesus and Zabbai.

"You greatly understated when you told me about this stallion," Adrianna said to John. "And, Michael, you didn't say anything about him at all," she scolded.

"We both knew you would recognize his greatness," Michael said. "Besides, there's no way I could have described him well enough. How about you? What will you say about him to the other horsemen?"

"I'll say that from the moment Zabbai came into view, I was held captive by his beauty and his presence," she said. "Then I'll share every detail of his perfection!"

"You win this time . . . " Michael said. "But if you think you've been awed by Zabbai, just wait until you meet my little Brother . . . the One Zabbai loves beyond all others. And wait until you see them together."

Shyly, her eyes downcast, Adrianna urged Tamir forward. "Hello," she said softly. Then she looked up, and all at once as their eyes met, her heart was full. Around them, time moved on. The horses stomped and snorted and munched at the sweet grass. The wind whispered through the tall trees that rimmed the meadow. Songbirds caroled to the clear sky. Squirrels chattered in noisy conversation. But Adrianna was held fast in the hope of tomorrow that shone from the young Boy's eyes.

Finally, Jesus spoke. "My mother and father will be so glad to meet you. Come, let us go to our home."

Side by side, the four riders moved smoothly across the meadow. Adrianna and her palomino walked beside Jesus and the dappled gray Zabbai. To the girl's right was Michael on Esdraelon. And on the meadow side rode John aboard a handsome chestnut gelding with a flaxen mane and tail.

Jericho and Larissa had been turned loose and now followed of their own accord, stopping now and then to taste the sweet grass, then jogging to catch up. Shadow loped happily through the trees near Jesus. Toward the sunset they rode, and only the muffled sound of the horses' hooves touching the cushioned earth disturbed the song of the meadow.

Near the main spring, a bull elk raised his head to survey the riders while his herd drank or ate contentedly. A curious raccoon peered at them from behind his comical mask. A

bright bluebird hitched a short ride on Jesus' shoulder, then flew ahead toward the camp. The inevitable ribbon of smoke wafted up from Mary's cooking fire, and the sweet odors of simmering herbs and spices beckoned the hungry travelers.

As the riders crossed the meadow, the elk bugled a welcome.

"Hello, my friend!" Jesus said with delight as they approached the huge animal.

"What's that?" Adrianna asked, with slight alarm.

Jesus grinned. "That's my friend, Magnus. See how high he holds his head, even with the weight of that huge rack he carries?"

"But I've never seen such an animal," Adrianna said, her eyes filled with wonder.

"There are many creatures here that will surprise you," Michael said. "And Jesus calls them all by name."

"I don't understand." Adrianna shook her head. "Where do these animals come from?"

"This is a magical place, not really like anywhere you've ever been," Michael said.

"There are other places in the world where there are many more of the forest creatures you'll see here," Jesus added. "This mountain retreat and these animals are special gifts from My Father."

"I have seen mountains before," Adrianna insisted, "but never a place or animals such as these."

"I think you'll enjoy the miracles that come with knowing Jesus," Michael said.

Joseph, who had donned his heavy woolen robe against the encroaching chill, walked toward the riders, happiness warming his rugged countenance. Behind him, Mary added vegetables to the pot from which the delectable odors issued.

The riders jumped down off their horses almost in unison and introductions were made all around. Soon John and Joseph were discussing politics and world events, while Mary and Adrianna became acquainted. Jesus and Michael tended to the horses, then joined the others for the evening meal.

Around the night fire, the friends visited. John explained the reason for his mission, sharing again the story Zadoc had told him. "With Herod gone," John said, "you can return to your homeland . . . though I can't imagine why you would want to leave this heavenly place."

Jesus sat quietly, stroking Shadow's head and taking in all that was being said. Close to the Boy, Adrianna played with the raccoon and the rust colored fox that were never far from Jesus and His dog. Michael gazed out into the night, appearing to be focused on something beyond the mountains. Only Mary and Joseph sat near John and listened to his tale with rapt attention.

"We must rest now," Joseph said when John had finished speaking. "There are decisions to be made, and this cannot be done in haste."

No one responded to John's comment about leaving their beloved home.

🐑

That night, a messenger angel visited both Joseph and Michael.

"You must return to your homeland," the angel told Joseph. "You will settle near the Sea of Galilee, in the land governed by Antipas. There, Jesus will continue to grow in stature and in wisdom until His time comes. His destiny must be fulfilled, and that cannot happen if you remain here. From now on, all of you will carry this place in your hearts and be strengthened by the memories."

To Michael, the angel said, "You will take this Family to Alexendria where they will board a ship and travel by sea to their new home. You cannot accompany them all the way to the land of their fathers."

"Why can I not go with them? Will they not need me wherever they go?" Michael asked plaintively.

"The wicked Archelaus is still a danger to Jesus," the angel answered. "The Roman soldiers assigned to his father have passed on the tale of the great horseman who aided in the first escape and it would not be safe for the Family to be seen in your company."

"But how will they make the journey alone, and where will they go?"

"They are never alone. The One God is always with them. Perhaps one day their destination will be revealed. But for now all of you will be safest if you cannot be forced to divulge their whereabouts . . . or tempted to seek them. Be at peace, Michael. A new life is soon to unfold for you. This part of your mission is nearly over."

⌒ MEANWHILE ON THE GREAT SEA ⌒

The ship's bow rose on a great swell, then dipped into a trough and nosed toward the next wave. Where the mist-paled sky met the sea, colors blended in monochrome shades of blue and gray. A strong wind urged the waters into a battle with themselves and the vessel that strained to cross them.

"I long to see beyond this boundless monotony," Luke scowled. "This is like being in a draped room with only mystery beyond its doors."

"Have faith, Luke. No sameness lasts forever," Archanus said, teasing but serious.

"What IS faith?" Luke asked.

"It's being sure of what we hope for and certain of what we cannot see."

"Is it faith that makes you go on believing that the Child born beneath the Star is indeed the Savior?" Luke asked.

"Yes, it is faith and~hope."

"Why hope if this Savior is for the Hebrews alone as I have heard?"

"He is for all people. The Hebrew prophet, Isaiah,wrote that this Son of God would also be a light for the Gentiles."

"Meaning?" Luke questioned, as a giant wave broke over the ship's bow, dousing the companions with cold, salty water.

"I think the Messiah will be the Light that guides those who are not of the Hebrew faith to the Truth of the One God."

"And away from the worship of idols and lesser gods?"

"Yes." Archanus was almost knocked off balance as the ship dove forward into the curl of another breaker.

"So what's in it for the believer?" Luke asked, undaunted.

"Life everlasting." Gripping a deck rail, Archanus spread his feet for better balance as the ship lurched and bucked.

"And you really believe in this?"

"Yes, I do," Archanus said. "as surely as I believe that this ship is riding high on a treacherous sea."

"But this faith is not logical."

"Must there be logic in all things?"

"The Greeks say there must."

"And what of their gods?"

"What do you mean?" Luke asked, staggering back when the ship surged up toward the crest of a monstrous swell.

"Are those strange beings in whom the Greeks place so much faith products of logic?"

"I see your point." Luke laughed.

"Never forget," Archanus counseled, "at the heart of everything is faith. And all logic, every equation, traces its heritage to some human assumption. Even the confidence that this ship will remain seaworthy relies on a form of faith."

"I hope your faith will save us from this angry sea."

CHAPTER
Eighteen

CHAPTER Eighteen

A deep chill gripped the morning air. A bank of low clouds rolled across the western mountains like a wave surging inexorably toward the shore. Birds huddled in their nests, unusually quiet, and the small forest creatures stayed close to their dens, sensing some unwanted change. In the meadow, the bull elk trumpeted mournfully, drawing the confused attention of his restive herd. The horses were alert and anxious.

There would be no regular gathering that day for the morning meal. Each of the players in this drama sought solitude to prepare for a parting that none could bear alone. In the little camp, all was quiet. Mary did not sing as she did most mornings, and between the men, there was no conversation. Michael had gone off alone on Esdraelon. Adrianna escaped to the private world she shared only with horses. Near the main spring, Jesus knelt in prayer with Shadow beside Him.

Only John sought companionship. Steam from the cup of warm liquid he carried mingled with the mist from his breath as he walked toward the clearing where Adrianna was carefully examining the horses. Beneath his warm woolen robe, he shivered involuntarily. As he drew nearer, he caught the sound of a muffled sob.

"Adrianna," he said from a few feet away, "do not mourn; all is not lost."

At the sound of the sympathetic voice, the girl turned and ran into the man's arms where she wept uncontrollably until she could weep no more. John held her and stroked her hair as one might hold a wounded child, waiting for the storm of emotion to pass.

Finally, looking up through swollen eyes, Adrianna asked, "Why must there be such pain in the world? Why can we not live simply in love? Why must we be torn apart?"

"Do you cry for Michael or for this Family?"

"I weep for them all . . . and for myself . . . and for you. I weep because there must be another parting in Michael's life . . . and because these good people face such uncertainty. I weep because when my eyes met those of Jesus, my heart was filled with something I cannot understand."

"There is a great mystery that surrounds this Boy," John said, drawing the girl closer, stroking the golden head that rested against his chest. "I believe that to look into His eyes is to see love in its purest and most magnificent form. And I think that we must not mourn the loss of Him. Rather we should thank the One God for the blessing of having known Him."

"But what of Michael?" Adrianna sobbed again. "These people have become his life, his family. How can he bear to lose them as he lost his own mother and father?"

"The One God will give him strength, and when he

returns to us, we will do all that we can to give him a good life and to console him."

"But what if he doesn't return to us?" Adrianna looked up at John again, her huge amber eyes imploring. "What if he is so broken that he goes off somewhere alone?"

"The One God will bring him back to us. You must have faith, you must trust Him."

❦

Two days later, a somber party began a long and uncertain journey. The morning light was cold and blue as the travelers set out, riding single file across the meadow. Each horse was heavy laden, carrying what goods they could for the expedition. The little dwellings stood forlorn and abandoned, even by the creatures of the woods that traveled in mute procession behind the entourage.

It had been decided that the camel and the donkey that had come with Mary and Joseph would remain with the wild creatures. Both were old and no one wanted them to be forced back into service in the hands of some unknown person who might not treat them with the kindness they deserved. Seeming to understand that they would not be traveling down the mountain, the unlikely pair walked slowly behind the elk and the deer on the way to bid farewell.

Michael and Esdraelon led the way, followed by Joseph, then Mary, Adrianna and John. Jesus and Zabbai were last in line, with Shadow leading the fox, the raccoon, the rabbits and the squirrels through the trees beside the meadow path.

No conversation passed between the riders, but when they reached the ridge, before they began their descent, they turned, almost as a unit for one last long look at their little paradise. No eye was dry, but no sound of sorrow broke the silence.

After a few moments, Zabbai stepped forward and Jesus dismounted. Falling to His knees His chin dropping to His chest, the Boy wept as around Him the air throbbed with unrelieved anguish. All the creatures He had loved gathered around Him, pressing against Him, nudging His arms, burrowing their tiny faces in His robes. The bluebird sat on His shoulder. The owl and the hawk ventured out of their tree top aeries to join their brothers in farewell. The elk and deer herds hovered anxiously. The mother bear and her cubs stood among the trees looking on.

At last, Jesus looked up and His heart reached out to embrace those He would not soon see again. After a while, all of the animals and the birds began to retreat back to their homes. Jesus climbed onto Zabbai's back and without a word, Michael turned Esdraelon and led the descent down into the canyon.

❊

That night they camped in the canyon at the foot of the switchback trail and made plans for the rest of the journey. John would go alone in search of a town where he could acquire camels. The others would remain at this well-hidden camp until he returned. It would be best, the friends reasoned, for Mary and Jesus and Joseph not to be seen in the city of Alexandria riding horses. But Jesus would ride Zabbai until the last possible minute, while camels conveyed Mary and Joseph and the Family's goods.

Upon John's return, he and Adrianna would head back with Larissa and Jericho to their winter pasture in the heart of the delta while Michael went on with the Family to the outskirts of Alexandria. In the city, Joseph would sell the camels and use the money to provide for his Family until they reached their destination and began a new life.

"We cannot accept your charity," Joseph had argued when John first outlined his plan to purchase the camels and the ship's passage.

"We have been sent by your God to help you," John responded. "Would you disobey Him?" And that ended the argument.

For the most part, they traveled in silence, making no great haste. The future loomed heavy before them and none was eager to hasten its arrival. Michael and Jesus often rode ahead; glad to be alone together, though they exchanged little conversation. Even the horses seemed melancholy, exhibiting none of the playfulness that was usually such a part of their great spirits.

Too soon the time came for Adrianna and John to head back into the heart of the delta where their families tended the herd. Since they left the mountain hideaway, Michael had scarcely spoken to Adrianna.

"You must talk to the girl," Mary admonished as John and Adrianna prepared to leave. "She is sure that you blame her somehow for this agony you face."

"How silly," Michael said scornfully. "This has nothing to do with her."

"Your anger is misplaced," said Mary. "We are all deeply saddened, and none more than Adrianna who thinks of no one but you."

"I'm sorry," Michael said, shaking his head. "It is just that I fear my own emotions. She is so tender, her sympathy so strong, that it is almost palpable. I have not been able to face my own possible response to her kindness."

"You must be the one to tell her this. You cannot let her leave thinking you have come to hate her."

So on the afternoon before John and Adrianna were to leave, Michael asked the girl to ride into the hills with him and for a few hours they were as they had been on the day of their first meeting. The palomino and the bay galloped side by side across the fields, then lunged together up the steep hills. When they reached the summit, the riders dismounted and turned the horses loose to graze and rest. For a long time, they sat together, looking down across the valley. Finally, Adrianna spoke.

"Will you return to us?" she asked, giving voice to the question that had been causing her heart to ache and filling her with dread.

"Yes, of course. Where else would I go?"

"Perhaps in search of your father."

"When the summer comes and we have taken the herd back to the northern mountains, then I may go in search of my father. But first, there is something else I must do. Adrianna . . . will you be my wife? When I come back, can we begin our lives together?"

"Is this a question you really need to ask?" Adrianna laughed and threw her arms around Michael's neck.

"Must you always answer a question with another?" Michael laughed back.

For a little while, their shared joy overshadowed the fear and the pain that had lain heavy on their hearts for the past several days. They talked of their future, of the children they would have and the horses they would breed. Michael told Adrianna of his mother, and his father, excitedly assuring the girl that Archanus would love her. When the shadows grew long, their hearts again turned heavy. Michael held Adrianna in a long embrace and they cried together, their tears mingling, flowing across the memories of yesterday and dampening the fertile fields of tomorrow.

That night they announced their plans to marry and there was much celebrating. At the center of the revelry, Jesus radiated the extraordinary joy that had not shown through His eyes since He said good-bye to the animals and the mountains.

As John and Adrianna prepared to depart the next morning, the women cried while the men exchanged a solemn farewell, John and Joseph understanding that they would not see one another again in this lifetime, Michael again assuring John that he would soon return to the horsemen's camp. Standing a little apart from the adults, Jesus looked on, an expression of unbearable suffering exposing the agony that gripped His heart.

For many miles there was only emptiness. The barren desert met the Great Sea on the north and spread its desolation far beyond the southern horizon. Following the seacoast, the wayfarers traversed the arid wasteland and for the first time ever, Michael was grateful for the lumbering camels that slowed their forward motion. For several days and nights they trudged, again mostly in silence. When they finally reached the place they would camp until it became time for them to part, there was no joy.

On the first night, Michael tried once more to convince Mary and Joseph that he should accompany them into the city of Alexandria.

"You don't know the way," he pleaded. "How will you find the harbor? And what if someone tries to harm you? Who will be your protector?"

"Our God will protect us and guide us," said Joseph, laying a gentle hand on Michael's shoulder. "We are no less downhearted than are you. But we must be cautious."

"I know," Michael sighed. "I know that you're right, that you must not be seen with me . . ." his voice trailed off.

"We can only pray that we will meet again," said Mary, reaching up to caress Michael's cheek.

"I have prayed for reunion before," Michael said, dispirited. "And never has your God seen fit to give me the answer I seek."

"In His time, dear friend, we will all come together again," Mary whispered, her voice catching on a silent sob.

For two days, they dallied beside the sea, camping in small a copse of willows, sharing stories and reminiscences, pretending against their fears and their sadness. It was Mary who finally summoned the courage to suggest it was time to move on.

Even in the desert, the morning light was cool. Waves drifted aimlessly against the shore of the Great Sea. A few errant clouds scudded across the eastern sky, their flat bellies assuming the warm and varied colors of the rising sun. A gull squawked noisily as it dipped and dove toward the sea, looking for easy prey. In the willows a dove sang its mournful song.

When Michael and Jesus returned to the camp carrying freshly caught fish for the morning meal. Mary took both of their hands and walked back with them toward the sea where Joseph sat looking out across the waters, silent and alone.

"It is time," Mary said when they were all together. "We cannot delay this parting indefinitely. Michael, you must begin your new life, as we must face our own."

No one else spoke. Joseph rose from his place in the sand and joined hands with the others. Jesus, standing now between Mary and Michael, raised His face to the sky and began to pray. Though His words could not be heard, their meaning entered the hearts of the others and a great peace at last settled over them all. Finally, He spoke. "Father in heaven," He said, "not our will but Thine be done." And it was over.

They ate, then prepared for their separate departures in silence. While Michael and Joseph packed the camels, Mary filled the fire pit with fresh sand.

Jesus went to Zabbai. The stallion lowered his magnificent head to rest against the Boy's chest and Jesus wept. Burying His face in the stallion's forelock, He let His tears fall without reserve.

The sun had broken over the horizon and slipped behind the subtle clouds that lingered still. From beneath that frothy bank, broad rays of light fanned out and spread across the land. Then, all at once, like the breath of God, one single brilliant shaft of light escaped the others and came to rest on the Boy and His horse.

From their place near the shore Mary and Joseph and Michael gasped together in awe of the scene before them. In a pool of glorious illumination, Jesus and Zabbai stood alone. No sound broke the silence, but the air was vital with the concerto of life. No one knew how long time was suspended . . . or if, indeed, it was. They only knew that when conscious thought returned, they were at peace and they could go on.

Soon they were traveling together, though apart, understanding that for them, there would never truly be a final parting. Their hearts would be everlastingly linked. Their memories would be as one. And finally, they would meet again in the time and place of the great beyond.

Riding toward the city, Joseph led the way on one of the camels, followed by Mary and Jesus on the other. Beside his master, Shadow jogged patiently. Headed south, Michael sat

astride Esdraelon and led Zabbai, who walked dejectedly, his head low, his step, for the first time ever, uncertain.

※

Two days later, on the prow of a great ship entering the harbor at Alexandria, two men faced the wind, rejoicing in the liberty of the moment, hopeful for the future.

"We will find him, Archanus," said Luke. "I know we will."

"I share your hope, my young friend, if not your assurance."

Disembarking from the ship an hour later, the companions looked around for some conveyance to carry them to their new quarters. But some great commotion held the attention of all those in the vicinity. The excitement centered around something on the dock near another ship that was preparing for departure to the northern ports.

"What can be the cause of all this excitement?" asked Luke.

"I don't know," Archanus answered with distaste. "There always seems to be some fuss in these cities. Come, we can walk a while. Surely we will find transportation away from this chaos."

"Why not go and see what's happening?" Luke asked, undaunted.

"I am sorry," said Archanus. "I don't mean to be unpleasant. But I'm tired from our journey, and the crowds only add to my exhaustion."

"Forgive my selfishness," Luke said, then looked up just in time to hail a passing carriage pulled by two fine horses.

"Can you take us to the University?" he asked the driver.

"Not the usual way, too much hubbub over there."

"What's going on?" Luke asked.

"Just some little family trying to board a ship," the driver answered. "People have been following them all through the streets."

"Why?" Luke wondered.

"No one knows." The man sounded perplexed. "I've talked with other drivers and men from the docks. It's a mystery."

Walking up beside the carriage a well dressed man overheard the conversation and joined in. "I heard they were some sort of royalty, but when I made my way through the crowd and got near enough to see them, I found everyone gathered around a simple peasant family . . . a man and his wife, their boy and his dog."

❧

The afternoon breeze had become a great wind. Large ships and small bobbed restlessly and tugged at their tethers. Low sun reflected off the brilliant blue of the sea and the white froth of the crashing waves. It was an ordinary afternoon, by city standards, until a subtle change of sound and sensation began.

The warm light of eventide breathed heavy across the land and the sea. A great crowd of people moved as a unit toward the dock. At the center of this wave of humanity, Mary and Joseph, Jesus and Shadow walked with silent confidence.

At first, the scene had reminded Joseph of the day he and Mary made their way toward the temple in Jerusalem to dedicate Jesus to the Lord. Passers by seemed to take note of his Family here, much as they had in Jerusalem nearly a decade earlier. And as it had before, a misty light seemed to surround them. The dust from the street rose in tiny golden particles around Jesus and Shadow, much as it had risen beneath the feet of the donkey that had carried Jesus and Mary into Jerusalem on that earlier journey.

"I do not understand," said Mary, sounding fearful.

"Nor do I," said Joseph. "But the crowd does not seem hostile."

"Perhaps there are angels with us?" Mary questioned.

"We are always in the company of angels, My mother," said Jesus touching Mary's hand, then walking on resolutely toward His future.

As they approached the dock, the crowd parted and the sea calmed. Looking around and shaking his head, the ships' captain dismissed the abrupt change of weather as a whim of the sea and urged the passengers to board so that they could immediately set sail.

"Come, come," shouted the captain. "We have taken on our cargo and only awaited the passengers."

Behind and in front of the Family a small line formed and soon everyone was on board. The gangplank was raised, and the ship made its way out of the calm harbor and onto the high sea.

❦

The next morning Archanus and Luke awoke early.

"I would like to go back to the docks today," said Archanus.

"Why?" Luke asked, surprised.

"I don't know. . . ." Archanus paused. "I've been uneasy since we left there yesterday. I should have listened to you when you suggested we go to learn the source of all the commotion."

"But we heard that it was only a peasant family."

"As are the people with whom my son has been living," Archanus sighed.

"Why didn't I think of that yesterday?" Luke all but shouted. "What was wrong with me?"

"Indeed. . . . What was wrong with us both?"

"We must be too late," Luke said, despair in his tone.

"Of that there is little doubt. But perhaps we can learn something, nonetheless. . . ."

In the chariot that was given to them when they presented letters from Zadoc and Diodorus to the prefect of the city, Archanus and Luke set off in search of the Savior.

***

At the prow of the northbound ship, Jesus and Shadow drank the wind, and looked hopefully toward an uncertain tomorrow, with Mary and Joseph behind them, but close by.

***

Toward the heart of the delta, Michael rode. Calling up the memory of his long ago epiphany and seeing once more the face of Jesus, he looked to the future and allowed himself to hope.

As the sun climbed into the heavens, the earth grew warm. As the day progressed, in the never ending cycle that is life, the dazzling light made its way across the sky toward another dusk, and then another dawn. The shadows lengthened and the air began to cool as across the Great Sea, a powerful wind gained momentum and the waves rose and crashed over one another in a great race to meet the land. Soon all the desert and the sea and the mountains far away rested in the blue-black light of a star filled heaven. And beneath that blanket, far apart, but oh so near, beat the hearts of those whose love would bind them together . . . on this long night, and forever.

EPILOGUE
Epilogue

What happens to the wanderer whose burden is a broken heart? Where does this traveler go to escape his deepest sorrow? In silence and solitude, he seeks his God. And one day, when his faith finds him and his strength is renewed, he journeys back to that place in the hearts of the ones God has sent to love him, that place that can only be called . . . home.

For many days after he parted from Jesus and the Family that had become his own, Michael roamed the countryside near the Great Sea. As it had at the loss of his mother and father, Michael's heart ached with a ferocity beyond endurance. His days were like melancholy dreams, seen in shades of gray and swept on by the winds of confusion. At night, in restless sleep, he was blown and tossed by waves of grief and despair that tumbled over one another toward the heart he battled to protect and the mind he sought to ignore. But God would not abandon this chosen one . . .

EPILOGUE

Epilogue

Through the dark night of Michael's soul, the river of God flowed inexorably, its healing waters washing away the desperation and nourishing the parched fields of the young man's tomorrows. Perhaps, in the end, he grew too tired to fight any longer with God. Or maybe his angel was at last able to breach Michael's wall of silence and throw open the gates of that prison to which the horseman had consigned himself.

Whatever the final undoing of his self-imposed exile, Michael began to emerge. Stepping out from behind the dark shadows that had blurred his vision, he could once again revel in the colors of the earth and the sky. Emerging from the tomb of his silence, he took comfort in the music of the wind and the waters. And in the aftermath of his awful isolation, he felt the love of God spoken to his spirit by the voice of Jesus.

On a brilliant morning, as the sun emerged in golden splendor and the waves of the Great Sea surged toward the shore, Zabbai raised his head for the first time since the parting and whinnied his greeting to the dawn. That day, the

travelers began their journey toward the future. Soon, they reunited with the horsemen. And before long, as Jesus had foretold, Zabbai began to sire fine horses, while Michael and his wife, Adrianna, gave life to wise and gifted children.

When his uncle, John, went home to be with God, Michael became the leader of his people. In that honored station, he guided the breeding of the horses, choosing the finest members of the herd to proliferate Zabbai's line. As time passed, it became known that horses related to Zabbai were uniquely intelligent, tractable and willing. Horsemen from all across the land sought to enhance their own herds with animals born to or descended from the herd over which Michael and his family presided.

Zabbai, as the One God promised, became the progenitor of the best and bravest horses the world would ever know. From a small nucleus, the descendants of Zabbai made it possible for mankind to explore and civilize the entire world.

With Jesus and Zabbai, the first true partnership of horse and human was born. Out of a Blessing given by the Christ Child beneath an awesome Star, the alliance grew. As Jesus and Zabbai shared the first years of their lives together in perfect love and understanding, a transformation occurred. A new affinity between horse and human had its genesis when the Spirit of Jesus moved that of Zabbai, forever altering the heart and the mind of the stallion . . . and all the horses that would descend from him.

Since, unlike Zabbai, Jesus left no blood heirs, the carrying on of His half of the partnership fell to Michael, His chosen brother. So it was that Michael and Adrianna, their children and grandchildren, began sharing the training methods of their people with those who came to acquire their horses. Thus it happened that ultimately the partnering of horse and human which began with Jesus and Zabbai changed the history of the world forever. And so it was that for over nineteen centuries, from modes of transportation, to beasts of burden and vehicles of war, the horse carried or pulled the human race into its future.

There is no end to this story. Wherever there are fine horses and admirable horsemen, the legacy continues. Down through the ages, the old ones have passed on the tale of Jesus and Michael and Zabbai, a Legend that was lost for a time . . . but not forever. Thanks to the keepers of the wisdom, we know that whenever the greatness of a horse or the mysterious genius of a horseman is so exceptional as to defy human comprehension, the horse is blood heir to Zabbai, the horseman, a descendant of Michael and Adrianna.

Will you know if one day you chance to meet such a miraculous horse, such an astonishing horseman? Perhaps. To learn the truth, you have only to look around for the best of the best. Then, reach out with your heart and hope for a glimpse of that meeting of spirits with which horse and horseman are occasionally blessed. In the moment you encounter these wonders, you will know and be glad that the Legend has been found . . . is true . . . and lives on.

❀

But what about Archanus? Will the Wise Man ever be reunited with his son? And will Michael ever again come together with Jesus and His Family? Well . . . that's another story. Perhaps you'll join us again, somewhere down the road~gather your loved ones around the night fire to read **Dawn Across the Mountains, Book Three of the Lost Legend Trilogy**~and learn the destiny of these people you have come to know and love.

N.A.R.H.A.
North American Riding For the Handicapped Assoc.

Because of Trilogy author, J. L. Hardesty's belief in the healing power of horses, a portion of the proceeds from the sale of every book in The Lost Legend Trilogy will benefit the

NORTH AMERICAN RIDING
FOR THE HANDICAPPED ASSOCIATION

N.A.R.H.A. is an organization that builds partnerships between horses and humans to help heal the spirits, the minds and the bodies of physically and mentally challenged children and adults.

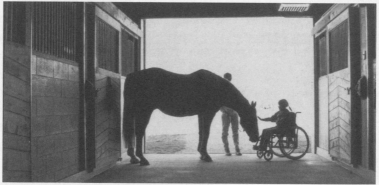

On a horse, someone whose disability prevents them from walking has the legs to run. Someone whose disability isolates them from others has a friend to trust. Someone whose disability impairs their balance has a way to regain it. And someone ~ anyone ~ whose disability presents special obstacles has the opportunity to overcome them. On A Horse . . . (N.A. R. H. A. ~ StirrUp Hope Campaign)

As a complement to this series and a way to further her efforts on behalf of N.A.R.H.A , the author has started an internet discussion group

www.horses4healing@egroups.com

Anyone interested in sharing or learning is invited to join this lively gathering of friends.

THE EDITOR
Marlene Bagnull

Marlene Bagnull is a gifted author, editor, teacher, and motivational speaker. She is the director of two major writers' events, the Colorado Christian Writers' Conference and the Greater Philadelphia Christian Writers' Conference. Marlene also teaches Christian writers' seminars around the nation and At-Home Writing Workshops, a correspondence study program.

The author of seven books, with more than a thousand sales to Christian periodicals, Marlene is a tremendous creative talent. She is a much sought after editor and a publisher whose company, Ampelos Press, is growing and gaining well-deserved respect.

For information on Marlene's availability as a speaker or on participation in one of her seminars or conferences, you may visit her website: writehisanswer.com ~ or write to her at Write His Answer Ministries ~ 316 Blanchard Road ~ Drexel Hill, PA 19026

THE ARTIST
Phyllis Waltman

Phyllis Waltman is a rising star in the world of equine art. She grew up on a farm and ranch on Colorado's rugged Western slope, totally absorbed with horses. From an early age she was both drawing and riding horses. For her, it was paper horses, rather than paper dolls.

Phyllis began working earnestly in the art world in 1981, depicting, of course, the horse. With precise yet sensitive detail, Waltman captures the expressiveness of these magnificent creatures.

Her work has received numerous awards and has appeared in shows across the country, including having been shown at the Churchill Downs Museum (home of the Kentucky Derby). In addition, her work has been the subject of features in EQUINE IMAGES MAGAZINE, THE ARTIST'S MAGAZINE (U. S. and Italian editions), WESTERN HORSEMAN, and EQUINE ART NEWS.

If you're interested in more information about Phyllis or her work, please send a note to the J-Force address on the following page.

IN APPRECIATION
Thank You!